D0455414

THE GREAT INLAND SEA

A NOVEL BY DAVID FRANCIS

THE GREAT INLAND SEA

A NOVEL BY DAVID FRANCIS

MacAdam/Cage

MacAdam/Cage
155 Sansome Street, Suite 550
San Francisco, CA 94104
www.macadamcage.com

Library of Congress Cataloging-in-Publication Data

Francis, David, 1957—
The great inland sea / by David Francis.
p. cm.
ISBN 1-59692-116-1 (alk. paper)
1. Australians—United States—Fiction. 2. Maternal deprivation—Fiction. 3. Mothers—Death—Fiction. 4. Horse grooms—Fiction. 5. Horseracing—Fiction. 6. Race horses—Fiction. 7. Australia—Fiction. I. Title.
PR9619.4.F73G74 2005
823'.92—dc22

2004030829

Manufactured in the United States of America.
10 9 8 7 6 5 4 3 2 1

Book and jacket design by Dorothy Carico Smith.

In Memory of Guggie Bright

PART ONE

I sit on the stone erosion wall watching Callie ride bareback in the early morning rain along Rehoboth Beach. It is September 1955, cool along the coast. She has on bathers and my coat. I pick up her Box Brownie and take a photo of her cantering through the shallows. The water splashes up around her.

She wears a plastic rain scarf, tied under her chin. Her mouth is slightly open. People think she smiles when she rides, but it's mostly determination. She sits perfectly still against the movement of the ocean and the horse's open stride. Instead of a saddle she has a burgundy blanket. The front of the blanket flaps back over her knees, the rest drapes out behind her, over the horse's loins. She likes to work them on the wet sand, the footing is solid. She likes the Delaware shore.

The leather camera cover feels smooth in my hand, there's green felt on the inside. Callie takes care of her camera. She fades from sight in the shore fog as she heads up towards the point. An old man walks a dog in the distance. I taste the salty morning rain on my face, swept in from the sea.

I keep the camera on the fog, wait for a shot of Callie as she comes back along the sand. The seagulls look big and primitive, the grey waves collapse quietly on the ordinary beach. I don't go down to the water, I watch it through the lens, focus and refocus, searching for her.

The straps were low and tight around my mother's long body, buckled to the wood-slatted base of the special bed. Her forearms, purpled with bruises, were bound in too. I knelt on the veranda bench and watched her through the fly-wired window, my chin in my fists, my elbows spread wide across the cool stone sill. I was twelve years old, small for my age. We lived in New South Wales.

She couldn't see me; the bed was angled wrong for it. My father had added a high latch and lock on the door, its brass knob luminous in the room's decay. The window was bolted so I couldn't get in. The moth-eaten drape was too short for the frame. It was two in the morning.

I knocked on the pane, softly so my father wouldn't hear. She strained her face and rolled her eyes to see. She knew it was me. A spoon-shaped palette was in her mouth, tied around the nape of her neck with a twisted tea towel. My father said it stopped her from swallowing her tongue.

I made random sentences to fit the number of bars on the bed to the letter, knowing there were seventeen. EMILY NEYDHARDT. I counted the letters on my fingers, added MRS to make them fit. Neydhardt was her name before she married and followed him there. The way she rolled her accent around the name. Her curious, deliberate English. When she was young, she was an opera singer in Vienna, but I'd never heard her sing.

The rods of the high-sided bed formed shadows that crisscrossed her. They dappled a pattern on the cream of the eiderdown. The moment when she'd usually struggle passed. No muffled cries, her body didn't jolt against the straps, just the murmur of the crickets. She was still. I squinted to see her in the faint light, my face against the glass. Her head lolled left towards me, her cheeks slack. She scared me the way she was. I clutched the small shining stone she'd given me, its rounded triangle in the shape of Tasmania felt smooth in my palm. A chill set in my toes.

Her blue cambric dress with the red flowers on it hung on a line, strung between the veranda posts beside me in the dark. I pulled the dress free of the pegs and wrapped myself in it for warmth on the hardwood bench. The fabric was frayed and thin from her days in the garden in the flourish of japonicas and jonquils she'd planted herself. She'd work the soil with her fingers, crusting her knees if she drew the dress up or wearing it threadbare if she didn't. The dress without ruffles or bustle, not navy or black like those of mothers with gardeners. Endlessly washed and wound through the wringer. The sun was so hot it faded a frock like that in a day. The roses had lightened from puce to pale pink, some fallen off on the way. Then she started to wash it overnight and hang it under the veranda; she'd put it on damp and unpressed in the morning. She got so she didn't press clothes. She didn't seem to care that her dress was the one she wore yesterday and the day before that. Or that it was wrinkled, uncollared, and unlike those of the women we'd pass in the street when we went in the buggy to town. She'd given up corseting, no longer wore stockings. She sometimes put on my father's shoes if she couldn't find her own, scuffing them unlaced in the dirt so she wouldn't step out of them.

Wound up in the dress, I slept on the bench. The latch of the door and my father through the window woke me. The bright-lit morning struck a fine sheet of dust across the room through the space between the sill and the bottom of the drape. I watched him unbuckle the leathers that strapped her quieted body. He undid the restraints on her arms and eased the tea towel coiled around her neck. He slid the palette slowly from her mouth. The pale grey of her open eyes.

He fluffed the eiderdown free of the depressions left by the tethers and pulled it up to cover her waxen face so there was none of her left to see. He walked over and drew the curtain closed, looked through me as though I wasn't there.

I moved deep into the agapanthus. He must have known I watched from somewhere. He had my mother wrapped in a hessian feed sack, propped up in the big wooden wheelbarrow, a shovel beside her. He bumped her down the steps. I kept low and tracked him, under the cypress hedge, out through the woven wire gate. He pushed her across the paddocks like a load of wood.

On the rise by the billabong he dug her grave deep and easy in the red sand. A few scrub cattle looked on. Done shovelling, he tipped her in from the side of the barrow. I felt the dull thump of her body as it met the earth, felt it in my hips as I lay flat as a lizard in the grass.

I watched her silent funeral through a failing windbreak of scant lucerne trees. On a rough-rutted stone he chiselled her first name and the year. He buried her in the middle of the mulga, a chicken-wire fence around the mound of earth.

My mother died with her eyes wide open in 1947, near Maude in the Riverina. No doctor was called, her body was not prepared. I still wonder what he was thinking as he dropped her in the dirt without a word or a coffin or the whole of her name, as he knelt and scooped red dirt to cover her with the chub of his pale Scottish hands.

I stayed in the trees all day, knotted on a branch, wearing her dress, and stared at the white, white sun. My father didn't find me. When it was dark I climbed down like something nocturnal. I went to Leonie's, I went there barefoot.

Leonie lived in the dust with a dog that didn't bark, in a mud brick hut where the river was unbanked and the floodplain spread. I watched her unsaddle a thin roan colt in the cool of midnight. She left it haltered, its saddle mark steaming, and came towards me through the shadows of the anthills. Her blood-red hair and snug-fit moleskin trousers, an old army bridle hanging from her elbow; its bit jingled as she walked.

"I like you in the dress," she said.

"My mother is dead." I said it offhand, like I might mention a horse looked lame. I thought she'd be surprised but she just hugged me hard, pressed her face in my matted hair and took me inside. I was too tired to tell her more. She didn't ask.

As she poured me leafy tea, I leant over the split-log trestle, my head held up in my hands. Her rangy dog licked dried sweat from my ankles and calves, blood from a scratch below my knee. I picked around weevils from a half of wheat cake as it crumbled in my fingers. It tasted like gravel, too dry to eat.

Leonie walked me to the canvas army bed, her long freckled arm to guide me. "Skin a rabbit," she said, trying to be cheerful. I raised my hands in the air as she slid the dress up over my head. It smelt stale and sweet. I lay down but I couldn't sleep. She didn't ask about my father.

She took the slush lamp, hooked it carelessly on a snapped-off sandalwood branch outside as she passed. The light wafted back and forth through the open door before it settled. It shed on her thighs as she slid from her trousers to bathe. The night air sagged around her. Her body was thin, but not as thin as my mother's had become. Leonie stood in the bucket to wash and an unlikely breeze quivered the flame of the lamp, dabbled the light on her breasts so they wobbled like flummery puddings. Her freckle-dotted stockman's tan left rings around her neck and forearms, the way granite meets sand, her sun-scorched arms like long gloves pulled up to her white shoulders. My mother's arms became pale, she was kept from the sun.

The day Leonie arrived, her face was already sunburnt from Far North Queensland. She came on foot, her hand through the reins of a footsore horse. She was handsome as boys from town, her red hair scooped up in a droop-brimmed hat. She had narrow brown eyes. I was ten.

My father hired her. She was supposed to be my governess, my mother couldn't seem to teach me any more. But Leonie couldn't read. She knew only horses, so she worked outdoors with my father. They rode out together like brothers, working cattle all day in the plains, walking in as night drew down around them, bearded in dust and talking in earnest. She lifted him from my mother like a rabbit from a cage.

The strangeness that came upon my mother was more gradual, a fungus up a tree trunk. When my father and Leonie headed into the desert, riding the boundaries, Mother set off after them. Walking with unstockinged feet, she tracked them through the thistles and sand.

From the veranda steps I watched as he realised she'd followed. He herded her home, bumping her forward with his horse's shoulder. He confined her to the house. With her silver pincers I pulled the splintered thorns of the bindi-eye from her purpled soles.

My mother lost her level and demanded that Leonie leave, so he shunted Leonie three miles up the river to the dusty, low-pitched hut, left her breaking brumby horses. He plotted his visits, announced he was going to town for bullets and barley when we didn't need a thing. When Mother walked to the cart to go with him in her white-ribboned hat for travelling, he shooed her back to the house like a following dog.

The night I was inventing eucalyptus tea in the shadow of the flowering gum, I saw Leonie and my father disappear through the chicken coop door. They didn't seem to care that Mother was up in the house. I put my eye to a nail hole. Her red gingham shirt was half undone and askew. He stayed clothed. Their bodies like jigsaw pieces, shadowed together, over and over, hay in her hair from the floor. The jerry-built shed pitched against me slightly as he buffeted her to the boards. My eye to the hole, my mouth against the tin. In the quickening movement a loose-nailed plank clattered free, its clenches risen. A hiss ran through his teeth as he slumped down on her, finished.

The rusty taste of the tin from the chicken coop wall came up in my throat as I lay in Leonie's bed and watched her through the doorway. She stood in the tub and dried herself. The lamplight played on her skin like gentle fingers.

I closed my eyes and saw my mother buried with her eyes still open. Did she land face down in the dirt or on her back, or did she fall in on her side? Artesian water seeps in that soil at night, brackish. Was the sack that wrapped her growing mould, soft-bodied worms disappearing inside the cerement, nudging at her skin already sodden from the dirt and night, searching for nooks to nestle in and breed? Her eyes were the lightest blue, dappled like shillings.

*

I woke at the bawling of a far-off calf. This was not my mother beside me. There was a dull whistle with each of Leonie's sleeping breaths. I traced the freckles on her milk-white back with my forefinger; a plump New Zealand and a funny-shaped butterfly. She smelt of damp grass. My mother's smell was different, softer. I would be without it.

The four-beat canter of my father's horse drummed up the track outside. I caught a hint of him through the open door at the tie-up as I skiffled out and slid beneath the bed among Leonie's scattered clothes. The dog lay on my mother's dress in the corner, snapping at flies and scratching its flank.

My father closed the wood-plank door behind him. "She died," he told Leonie without particulars. Leonie said nothing; she already knew. I hadn't heard my father speak since he had locked my mother in the room. He sounded different with Leonie, less Scotch.

"I had to bury her," he said, undressing, his pants on the floor. "Have you seen the boy?" He didn't call me by my name. Leonie didn't say, but she often didn't answer. "I need to keep him to the house," he said.

I lay as still as a stone. The dog on my mother's dress was on my father's blind side. I prayed he wouldn't see it. Leonie had him occupied; we all conspired in pairs.

Their bodies shadowed on the canvas above me, but I couldn't see them. I'd never seen my father naked, he'd never let me. I wondered why she fancied him. His movements against her pressed me to the floorboards, the dusty underbelly of the bed smudged against my chest. They seemed more coupled from their hips than at their mouths. As his body stopped and slumped, an arm fell loosely over the edge of the bed like the limb of a dead thing, his hand so near my face I had to move and risk a sound.

My father's name is Darwin. He has one lazy-lidded, hooded eye. An eye that belongs to another man's face. A mickey bull kicked up at him, the branding iron was in my hand. When the swollen purple subsided, it uncovered the colour of a bloodshot potato. He couldn't see out of it.

I look through the camera, watch for Callie. The fog shifts along the waterline, bits of it lifting. I wait for the steel-grey legs of the horse, like the colour of the ocean, the white of its body, the colour of the air, but they still don't appear. She doesn't usually take this long. I get down from the ledge and look up the beach to see if she's coming.

Callie walks along the sand on foot, she looks small in her meadow-green bathers. She doesn't hurry. There is no sign of the horse. The plastic rain scarf has fallen down around her neck, her hair is wet and sticking up. She doesn't have my coat.

She shouts something, but she's out of earshot, her words get swallowed in the sound of the waves.

"Where's the horse?" I ask when she gets close.

"I took him swimming but I couldn't turn him 'round," she says. She clasps her hands close to her chest. "He kept going straight out, head up like he was bolting. I had to get off and let him go."

She has goose bumps on her shoulders—she doesn't usually feel the cold. I don't ask her where my coat is.

"There's nothing you could have done," she says.

I've never seen a horse get the better of her, not on dry land. She says swimming a horse a hundred yards is worth a mile's gallop.

"He'll probably come back in," I say. I look out to sea. A grey lump lolls on the waves not far out and we watch as the horse washes up and lands on the beach. His head lies flat on the sand, set straight from the end of his neck, his legs stick out like fence posts.

"I wonder where he thought he was going," I say as we go down.

Callie walks close to me for warmth. I'd give her my coat if I hadn't already. The horse still has his bridle on; the reins didn't break, they loop on the beach. The waves lap at his belly, leave lips of froth as they recede. A dog keeps rushing down and barking, running backwards up the sand. The horse has seaweed in his tail.

A car stops along the foreshore road and an elderly couple get out. I shrug my shoulders at them, pretend it's a mystery.

"We should call someone," I say to Callie.

"He'll be covered by the high tide," she says.

She goes down and kneels by the horse's head. Seawater runs to her knees and into the dents they make in the sand. For a moment I think she's about to do something like close his eyes but she undoes the throatlatch and eases the bridle over his ears. The cheek strap pulls at his eye as the buckle slides down his face. I don't help her. She unclips the cavesson noseband, tries to lift his head to get the other side free. Dead horses are heavy, especially their heads. His mouth is closed around the bit. There's a screech of metal as it snatches against his teeth when she removes it. The couple watch us from back inside their car.

Callie holds up the bridle, sorting out the reins.

"It'll be fine with some Murphy's Oil," she says.

We walk in silence up the beach, past the stone erosion wall, towards Callie's two-horse trailer. My coat, washed up with a bundle of seaweed, lies on the sand. I pick it up and untangle it, wring it out. I pretend not to notice the couple in their Plymouth as we pass.

Callie drives home in her green bathers. The plastic scarf lies down around her neck; her hair stands up at angles. I put my hand on her leg. Her body is warming up even though the car is cold. The salty bridle sits on the seat between us, my wet leather coat on the floor. The trailer behind us rattles and bounces without the weight of the horse.

"Was it scary?" I ask her.

"I'm not scared of the water," she says.

"I mean when you couldn't control him."

She grips the steering wheel tight so her knuckles look bony; her thigh is tense under my fingers. She only looks at the road. "He wasn't going to be an important horse," she says.

My mother was married with a garland of cream gardenias threaded across her brow. I saw a faded photo. She was standing alone, by a fountain in the snow. She married him in Vienna. She was nineteen and he was thirty-six. He had travelled the world. She said he was almost handsome then, before his eye was done in. She was with her family, they came to hear her sing. He promised he'd only take her for two years. She didn't know it took three months to get there.

He went on ahead, said he wanted to find her the perfect place. Then he wrote her with instructions to follow. He told her it was beautiful, the climate was warm, there were kangaroos. She was pregnant but he didn't know. It was 1935.

Twelve weeks on a steamer via the Cape of Good Hope. She had me on board the boat, halfway there, a chair and towels on the deck, she said, somewhere off Mauritius. She waited a month in Melbourne, went by train to Echuca, then overland in the heat and dust and blistering of lips, on horse, then camel, then bullock-drawn carriages, a buggy, then a dray. The roads were too rough for the cars they had then; my mother didn't drive.

I imagine her seeing it, weary in the afternoon as she came upon the place, me feeding on her. Her chafing breast gone dry in the travelling. Two rows of rooms on a rise in the middle of the scrub, the roof thatched above rough mud bricks and sandstone, a few slat-ribbed cattle per square mile. A marginal spread of spinifex and sand, measured in days' ride or miles square, too many acres to count.

Almost a year since she'd seen him, she stared into the red of the desert's distance until it bloomed an orange dusk bearing far-off men on rough, brumby horses. A round-faced, hooded-eyed man on a buckskin, the feckless Scot she'd followed. Watching him appear, a little too pink for this part of the world, not enough chin. The stockmen riding in with him looked more the part. Broad-brimmed hats shading sharp, weathered faces, the tan of their skin drawn tight.

She said the place was nothing like he'd promised. She said he didn't take me from her, didn't want to hold me in his arms.

My father called me The Creeping Jesus. After seeing him with Leonie on the bed above me, I scraped through a space between fallen boards in the corner of the hut. He didn't see me leave.

I ran back through the scrub to the house, crawled in the sewing room window, but the lining of my mother's hatbox was empty, her money for "when we are going" was gone. My father had been there, I could tell by the way the lid was left open and the silk of the lining was torn. His house dog watched me from the door.

My legs were being spotted with the bites of mosquitoes and sand fleas. To cover them I took the dust-coloured nankeen trousers thrown on the compost heap by the Chinese cook my father had fired. I washed them in the cement sink in the outside laundry, with a pumice and purple soap, scrubbed them of the colours of cooking. I rinsed and fed them through the wringer, forcing the turn of the handle from a bucket I stood on, like nights I helped her with the dress. The legs flattened into wrinkled tongues.

I put them on to dry, folded down their tops. I wrapped a stirrup leather twice around my middle, rolled up the trousers five times at the bottoms and stowed my stone in a slot in the pocket that was meant for a penny. I liked the way it felt against my thigh.

I heard my father coming home, cantering up the drive in the half-light. I crept into the cover of the powder-lit garden gone wild since my mother's confinement, closed the ivy-cloaked meat safe door behind me. Mould and sweating leather reminded me of the smell of curing sides of beef that hung from the ceiling hooks; my father used to slaughter there, but not anymore. I was hidden.

My father had put my mother's clothes in a tea chest in the corner of the meat safe when he stopped letting her outside. Her Christmas socks with red-hatted rabbits holding hands around their tops became plumper as I pulled them tight over my calves. I tugged on her jodhpur boots, tied the too-long laces in a double knot around their backs. I never wore socks, hardly ever shoes. But I couldn't stop the freezing in my feet.

A wrought-iron bath was stored unplumbed against the wall. Narrow and deep with rusted, lion-clawed feet. I lay down in it, her dress wound up as a pillow, her musty smell, and waited until morning.

I woke to a shadow behind me. I sensed it was my father, but as I turned, the door whined closed. He locked it and was gone. I got up warily, folded the dress in an Arnott's biscuit tin with my other special things, hid them under the old milk separator. He'd locked the door but not the window; it hadn't rusted shut. I twisted my head and slid on my back, threaded through the inches piece by piece, scraped the side of my face on the sill. I could get places a boy shouldn't fit. My father once said I had snake hips; it was all a matter of angles.

I walked stiff-legged past the stables, hushing the cattle dogs. The pony in the paddock was startled by my movement in the half-light, snorting steam and trotting, his tail up over his back. I cornered him near the shed, kept the dogs from chasing.

The front-room lamp beside my father's leather sleeping chair was the only light the distance carried. I looked over my shoulder, watched the light shrinking as I got further away.

If she slept on her side, she said she had nightmares. Then he kept her in the room, wheeled in the special bed and trussed her into it each night on the wend of her spine, her head facing up. He said he didn't want doctors or hospitals, he thought he could treat her himself. She hardly seemed to sleep after that; she woke against the restraints when she did. The palette gagged her silent but for the sucking sounds. I watched her through the nailed-up window.

My mother had polio as a child; it curved her spine just slightly. She walked with one hip higher. They said she shouldn't have children. She only had me. My name is Day.

Callie drives faster than usual, she doesn't look at things as we pass. We cross into Maryland, closer to home. There are fields of corn on either side. The empty horse trailer tows lightly behind us, it floats around the corners. She doesn't talk about the horse drowning.

"What'll you tell Mrs. Voumard?" I ask her.

"I'll tell her he couldn't swim," she says.

The tide will be rising by now, picking the dead horse up from the seaweed and washing him back and forth against the foreshore wall. He'll float again.

"I can't swim either," I tell her.

"You didn't grow up around water," she says.

"Neither did the horse," I say. I put my foot up on the glove box and look at the trees.

"Do you ever think about dying?" I ask her.

"I'll have time to think about that when I'm dead," she says. She concentrates hard on the road. "My father's had time to think about it," she says.

"What do you mean?" I ask. She's never mentioned him.

"He's been dead six years," she says.

I don't ask her what happened, she's already driving too fast. Out the side window there's a field being harrowed, a man with a pipe on a tractor.

"I don't know if mine's still alive," I say. When I think of him dead it's dragged from a horse through a tussocky paddock, his foot twisted up in the stirrup, the side of his face bumped through the sand then draped in the dirt as the horse stands still at a trough. "He's probably dead by now," I say. "He had an infected eye."

"You don't die from an infected eye," Callie says.

"People die from strange things there," I say. I reach down and touch the jacket on the floor; the leather's still wet. I wring out an arm but only get a drip. "I think my jacket shrunk," I say. I imagine the horse reefing out into deeper water, Callie struggling free from the coat to swim in alone. I wonder if she stopped and looked back.

"Do you really not care about the horse?" I ask.

She doesn't like being quizzed, I can tell by the set of her jaw and the way she stares at the road.

"There's nothing I can do about the horse," she says. She rubs the window with the back of her hand. The camber of the road drags us into a bend.

"It looked big on the beach," I say. I watch her short, chaff-coloured hair, her eyes fixed on the asphalt.

"Haven't you ever seen anything dead before?" she says.

"Not lately," I say. Callie doesn't speak. "My mother once tried to teach me to swim," I say. I look at the bridle between us.

"People who can't swim annoy me," she says.

I hitch an arm of the jacket in the window and wind it shut, to let it dry outside. I listen to the wet leather flap against the car, the buckles banging on the paint. It feels like the horse trailer might get airborne.

"Why do you pretend you don't care?" I ask.

"Because people like you pretend that you do."

"That's bullshit," I say. I pull the coat back in the window and hold it in my lap. "Can you let me out?"

She puts her foot further down and goes even faster. "Let yourself out," she says.

I didn't know exactly that I was leaving, but I knew I wasn't coming back. I rode out on Muddy Gates Lane, slumped in the saddle, too hungry to think. A crowd of emus fanned into the plain from the shade of gum trees, their heads and feathered tails bobbing, a wisp of pink where a piece of sky was broken.

In Maude, the local dogs were up and barking but the townies were sleeping in their beds. I knocked at the doors and windows of Cova Cottage, hoping the Appletons might wake and give me food, but there was no sign of life in there. I helped myself to plums the magpies hadn't fed on in their yard.

A few miles out on the Damascus Road, twenty miles south of where I'd come from, a cattle drover was making breakfast with a tin billy by a fire. His border collies skulked around the edges of a hundred head of sheep as they grazed beside the road. I tried to pass unnoticed, to get further away, but the stock horse whinnied when he saw me.

"Wanna cuppa?" The drover waved me over.

I tied my pony up beside his horse, but not so close that they might kick. I ate the jam and damper like I'd not seen food all year, poured from the billy into a can that carried meat. The hot tea in my throat felt like honey.

"How's ya lovely mother?" the drover said. I didn't expect he'd know me. "I seen ya walkin' with her down the town."

"She's poorly," I said.

Before there were more questions, I got up and went. By the time I hit Deniliquin it was already afternoon and I was feeling halfway better, the pains of hunger passing, but it was thirty miles further and the pony was footsore. I got off and laid my hands around his hooves, felt the heat in them; his soles were bruised by stones.

There was a blacksmith on the edge of town working at his forge. The smell of freshly burnt hoof as he put a too-small shoe on a draught horse and rasped the foot to fit it. I knew the shoe should fit the hoof, not the hoof the shoe, but I didn't mention it.

"I don't have any money except my pony needs to be shod," I said, deepening my voice like I was older.

"Won't do shoes for nothing," the man said, Irish.

I watched and waited. It looked bad to lead a limping pony through the streets. When the farrier finished the heavy horse, clipping the ends of its clenches, he stood up slowly, his hand in the small of his back. He took a good look at my bush pony.

"I'll give you fifty quid for him," he said, "shoe him for myself."

It was a lot of money for after the War. The pony was a good one but I had to get to where it was green like Europe.

"How much for the saddle?" I asked him.

"Nothing," he said.

I undid the girth and put the poley saddle over my arm, took the dirty notes from the Irisher's blackened hands and counted them. I'd never seen so much money.

Four pounds three shillings bought a sit-up-all-night ticket on the Riverina, overnight to Melbourne. It left me with two twenties and a fiver, a bunch of shillings clinking in my fingers, and a saddle on my arm.

I hadn't travelled on my own before. The train shunted and squealed and let off steam. I slept with my hand around the rolled-up money, dreamt of my father rustling and snapping at kindling, tearing and balling up pages of old telephone books as he stoked the boiler with a blackened poker, his hands ingrained with the sand that lay in the furrow of his brow, settled in the spit on his teeth.

I woke up sweating, my reflection in the black train window, nothing outside but night. I looked grubby compared with people propped up in their seats around me. I borrowed a towel from the top of a sleeping lady's bag, took it to the bathroom where there was soap wrapped up in glossy paper. I shut the lid of the lavatory because it smelt and the rattle of the tracks was loud up through it. I wet my hair and washed it in the basin. I rubbed the suds over my body and cleaned out my dusty mouth. I washed my clothes in the water I poured for my hair, pushing at them in the basin until the water was sandy brown. I didn't have underpants but I still had my mother's Christmas socks.

I rolled my wrung-out clothes in the train lady's towel,

plopped them on the lavatory lid, and stamped them dry. Standing naked in the cold, I slid the window open and watched the trees go by. I'd never seen a forest. I held the towel, my shirt, and pants out the window, let them dry in the train wind, careful not to lose them to the night. A man kept knocking at the door but I didn't let him in.

A lurching stop without a station, the sound of train men yelling and the carriage standing still. Sheaths of daylight came in through the window. A racehorse farm with creosote yards of thoroughbreds in clover, the grass a green I'd never seen.

I took my saddle and moved along the aisle through the cabins, my clothes still damp against my skin. Shelter sheds and a sandy galloping track. I jumped with my things and walked down the railroad siding towards them as the train ground off and squawked behind me.

A scrawny stable boy not much bigger than me was pouring buckets of grain in feeders. I put my children's saddle down behind a painted shed.

"Where's the owner?" I asked him.

"Mr. Delauney." The boy pointed to a red-faced man with a pipe against the post-and-rail track watching horses gallop.

"Do you need a rider?" I asked the man.

"Where did you appear from?"

"Off the train. I'm a jockey from the bush. I won the Birdsville Cup." It was the only race I'd heard of.

He let me ride a chestnut two-year-old in a round white yard. "Someone help Train Boy with his things," he said to a groom. Delauney didn't ask me for my name. I wondered if I'd fooled him into thinking I was a jockey, or if it was obvious I was twelve years old.

Six years I worked for M. L. Delauney at Sutton Grange. I broke and galloped the young thoroughbreds, cleaned out straw, and fed out hay to his brood mares. I learnt to gag their mouths and file their teeth; I rode his jumping horses. If I made myself too tired to think, I could sleep without dreams that would wake me. If I slept sitting up, it was a primeval man who would run through the trees, his coat sprouting manes of dark horses, or sometimes it was my mother in clay.

I went as a groom with a horse to America. It was 1953. The horse was called Unusual. He was a five-year-old; I was eighteen. Neither of us had been to the docks before.

I hadn't thought of America, but that's where the horse was going and I was the one who could handle and ride him.

Standing in my overalls at the West Melbourne wharves, my fingers through the horse's headstall, his chestnut tail backed into the drizzle, I checked the pile getting wet beside me. Six bales of straw, three of lucerne hay, Unusual's lucky racing bridle, a New Zealand rug and Epsom bandages, three bags of chaff and crushed-up barley, a kit of liniments. In my pocket I felt for the envelope with the livestock export papers. I pulled them out and looked again at the address: Thomas H. Shackelton, Lower Wye Plantation, via Easton, Maryland, USA. I had my knapsack on my back, exercise saddle at my feet. All I didn't have was a passport for myself. I never had a birth certificate, I was born at sea.

Canvas straps were roped around the horse's girth and loins. It was as though his eyes were out on sticks. I was worried too. His legs hung stiff beneath him as they hoisted him up and landed him among the solid freight. He skated around the greasy deck before he found his legs.

"If that horse goes bonkers, I'll have him shot," the captain shouted through the rain.

I ran up the sea-soaked ramp, approached the horse both quick and quiet to calm him. I had a syringe in my pocket, but only half a shot of tranquilliser. I would save it for the worst.

Unusual was a steeplechaser out of a Devil's Elbow mare. His sire was called Untouchable. Delauney had sold him to a rich American to race him over timber. He was insured for ten thousand pounds, bought for more than that.

I didn't travel well. There was no provision for me on the boat, it wasn't set up for passengers; the horse's new owner hadn't paid for me to be on board. The cook left me cans of army meat and a tin spike at the bottom of the poop deck stairs. I slept huddled against the feed on the only piece of floor that didn't slosh with water when the vessel pitched and sloped. A biliousness swept over me, the taste of salt in the stale bilge air. But I had left Australia. I always knew I would.

By way of celebration I ran upstairs and vomited, followed it through the wind. It was easy to believe there was no land behind me when all I could see was ocean. But below the swoop of gulls, the chop still made me queasy. I went back down to sleep on a bed of stale hay.

The third night out, I harpooned a rat with a pitchfork and threw it out the door. On the fourth, the wooziness got worse, I had the runs and chundered until my insides hurt. I primed the syringe and stabbed myself from behind with a squirt of milky tranquilliser, the pain of it shot to my teeth.

*

When I woke, I couldn't tell if it was the next day or the one after that. Unusual was climbing the walls of his narrow clapboard stall, trying to lie down; his legs were swelling badly. I took his temperature; it had crept above a hundred. Horses can't vomit, they can get colicky and die with a twisted bowel. Days and nights I kept the horse standing, massaged his legs with soap and water until my hands were crippled with cramps. I mixed in Penetrene, made salt-water poultices, stole frozen meat from the freezer up in the galley that I bandaged around his shins and fetlocks. The smell of rubbing alcohol and putrid meat, vinegar and eucalyptus, horse piss acrid in the straw. Out the only porthole I saw a submarine, which followed the ship like a smooth-swimming dolphin. I hoped it wasn't Russian. I didn't tell the captain, I was afraid he might turn back.

Twenty-six days later we arrived at Long Beach Harbor. U.S. Navy ships were tied up in rows like well-fed horses, their decks filled with men in sailors' uniforms. I had lost a stone in weight in transit. I got ashore because Unusual went berserk on the pier when a crane swung something past him. I ran the plank and took the lead rope from a nervous-looking longshoreman.

The customs agent trucked me and the thoroughbred into three weeks' quarantine, in case we'd brought in rhinoviruses or other horse diseases. They kept us somewhere near the Los Angeles airport, behind a chain-link fence. It felt good to be far from my father.

"Why you here without papers?" the customs agent asked me.

"Got to look after the horse," I said.

"You need to do better than that." He laughed, imitating my accent. He'd fought with Australians in New Guinea, said he'd been to Brisbane on R and R. He signed the papers and said I was lucky. Get a passport, he told me.

The seasick racehorse looked much better, and I was better too. We went by truck to Union Station, on a goods train to Baltimore, in a straw-filled carriage to ourselves.

Near a town called Needles, I saw a herd of mustangs running, frightened by the train. At Flagstaff, travellers gathered on the platform as I curried out the horse's winter coat. I gave a girl a tuft of chestnut hair. She asked if I was going to the Grand Canyon.

"You can ride down it on a mule," she said, looking at Unusual.

"This is a racehorse," I told her.

In Wichita, Kansas, I was given a hamburger and french fries. The funny way people talked, all enthusiastic. I had a railway map so I knew where I was going. So many towns, there weren't enough names. Eight states with a place called Paris. One was in Kentucky. Out the window there were farms forever, racehorse studs, grasses that would make a fat pony founder. I wondered what would happen if Americans owned Australia.

When we got to Philadelphia, I saw a black family who looked like they lived on the seats at the station. Then the train separated from the carriage beside me; my half went south to Baltimore, the rest went on to New York City.

Lower Wye Plantation had the biggest house I'd seen: columns in front and three storeys high in the middle. Brush-filled jumps in post-and-rail fences separated crops of corn from fields of sheep and timothy. A sunken fence they called a ha-ha ran across the lawn, down to the river. Watermen worked in the shallows where the Wye River widened and narrowed from Chesapeake Bay. I saw a walled fruit garden full of figs. It looked like I imagined Europe, as though my mother might have lived there. It was the Eastern Shore of Maryland.

I watched Thomas Shackelton walk down to the stables in his barn-door-fronted jodhpurs, a flap and buttons up one side. He seemed more enthused about the arrival of the horse than the rat-haired boy who came with it. I asked if I could school Unusual over jumps. When I galloped a hawthorn row and a stile out into a sheep field, he offered me fifty American bucks a month and board, a slope-roofed hut by the barking pack of foxhounds. A smile went up the side of my face. I didn't mind that I wasn't expected; I was glad to be where it was green and there were hedges, lawns, and sprinklered gardens.

The leaves had turned and some had fallen. It was fall instead of long, hot spring, fall instead of autumn. I lay in a field and looked upwards, felt the moist breath in my chest. My mother had been gone for almost seven years.

When I was still, I wished she was with me, that it was my father who was dead.

Now is the time of day I wait for; Callie comes around on Sunday evenings. It's been a week since the young horse washed up dead. We haven't spoken since. I lie down on my bed in the hut that Tom Shackelton gave me and watch out the door for her car on the Wye River Road. The roof slants low above my head, the rain makes patches of damp in the wood. It's my second September here. I've made it kind of comfortable even though it's small and mostly dark bare boards. There used to be shelf beds but I took them out. Someone said they were once for slaves.

A car rumbles by but it isn't Callie. The foxhounds in the kennel scrape their plates on the cement. Feeding them is my last job for the day. Once they're done they pace and whimper; the damp night makes the scent of deer and vixen strong. If I had a car, I could go out and find her.

It's nearly two years since I met her, since I bumped towards the main gate on the stable bike, my first time off the place. The front wheel had a rim that was warped and moaned with each turn of the spokes. The leaves on the chestnuts had turned and fallen, left them bare like naked men.

I was looking for tar roads I could walk the young horses on, harden their tendons and pasterns with slow work on the asphalt. On gravel they can bruise their soles;

on the grass verges it's rough, their tendons can bow, fetlocks get sprained.

Around a bend a tall, slack-limbed black girl stood on the roadside facing a clapboard shack, her hands held up in prayer. Hearing the groan of the bike, she let her arms hang loose from her shoulders and stepped into a slowed-up walk as if nothing was doing. Half a furlong past her, I looked back over my shoulder. She stood still, she was praying again.

A gappy-toothed boy in dungarees was selling lemonade from a box in a gateway, a shanty set back in the trees behind him. 1 NICKLE it said on a board in the grass. "What's she doing?" I asked him, pointing back at the girl. He didn't say, just looked away like he couldn't speak.

At the next crossroad a group of negroes surrounded a car under a big oak tree. A crop-haired white girl stood on the running board, her skin seemed to shine in the sun. She smiled like she knew she was doing something she wasn't supposed to. Her hand was on the shoulder of a man with a dark purple face, wearing overalls and a peaked tweed cap.

Men were wandering up from a hayfield to see what was going on. "Two-to-one, Hoofers can't clean jump the hood of this automobile," she shouted, pointing at the bonnet of the car and admiring the man who was Hoofers. She was wearing tiny lace-up paddock boots and balloon-topped jodhpurs with a zipper in the front like a boy's. She was a jaunty sort of girl.

Lookers-on mumbled among themselves; it was a hump-fronted Chevrolet, high in the middle; mudguard to mudguard it must have been seven feet wide. I wondered if I could jump it on a horse.

The jumper threw his hat down on the ground and people put in coins, announcing the amount as they dropped them. "Dime." "Three quarters." "A nickel," from the lemonade boy who'd come down the road and found his voice. When everyone who was going to had offered up a bet, the one called Hoofers walked backwards up the tarmac, measuring strides like he was at the Olympics, except he had on overalls. He stopped at fifteen paces, turned around and spat on his hands, hurtled down towards the car, and jumped it easy, both knees bent up and flung to one side. He landed barefoot on the hard tar road.

The girl picked up the winnings, poured the coins into her jodhpur pocket, threw the hat in through the window, and got in the car. She drove with Hoofers beside her, except she was like the chauffeur, looking out through the hoop of the steering wheel.

I waved at them to stop. He was counting the takings on the seat. She rolled down the window. "Do you ride horses?" I asked her. I could tell she did by her clothes.

"Jumpers," she said, "for Mrs. Voumard over on the Choptank. I'm going to be a woman jockey."

"What's your name?"

"Callie," she said, "Coates."

"Her real name's Calliope," said Hoofers and laughed behind his hand.

"Can I put the bike in the boot?" I asked. She got out to supervise the loading. "This is America and this is a trunk," she said as she opened it, "and that's a girl's bike you're riding—it's got a basket on the front." I liked her already, she was full of the devil.

"Women aren't jockeys," I told her. "I never saw a woman riding races."

"Hoofers is my groom," she said.

I got in the back seat. The car was plush with wood inside. Hoofers had his hat back on his head. "Four bucks and a quarter," he said.

"Whose car?" I asked.

"Mrs. Voumard's," she said. "She sleeps in the afternoons. Which way?"

"Go straight. I work at Lower Wye. I rode races in Australia," I said, but she didn't seem impressed.

We passed corn and safflower fields, and then a sweep of black-eyed yellow flowers. "What are they?" I asked. She looked at Hoofers and they laughed.

"Sunflowers," she said. "We feed the seeds to the horses. It shines their coats like wax."

"Where I am, the fieldworkers have fighting cocks," I told them. "They train them for combat, wrap their hands around their clipped wings, run them back and forth on an old spring mattress to get them fit." I got the feeling they already knew about cockfights.

We approached the lank figure of the girl in the spotted frock. "I saw her before," I told them, pointing as we passed. "What's she doing?"

"Prayer walking," Hoofers said in the drawl of the Eastern Shore. "Places get burnt 'round here; you have to get them prayed over."

We passed a little field where the ground was all humped and sunken, cobbled with gravestones pitched in the ups and downs of the dirt.

I leant forward, my chin on my hands on the high bench seat between them. Callie caught me glancing at her in the rearview mirror; she met me there with a smile in her eyes. I felt squeezed up inside, a wave of colour spreading over my face.

"I know a horse could jump this car," I said.

It was nine forty-five at night and cold, waiting with Unusual among the roadside oaks for the rumble of the Chevrolet. Headlights approached in the fog and stopped. We loaded him quick and quiet onto Mrs. Voumard's two-horse trailer and travelled. I drove because Callie and Hoofers didn't have licences; I didn't either, but they said it was better because I wasn't from there.

We trundled east through a town called Reliance that didn't have lights, over the border into Delaware towards a place called Blades, where no one knew us. We parked under a dim streetlamp near a backwoods barn where Hoofers said the cockfights were. We could hear the muffled voices and scuffling birds as we unloaded the horse. The night was black as bitumen.

I got up on Unusual and headed back down the road. In the cover of woods, I kept him warm and ready. He had a sheepskin shadow roll around his noseband and a netted neck and body blanket. He was dressed like a jousting steed, covered from his poll to the dock of his tail so no one would remember him. He was running over timber in the Maryland Hunt Cup that coming Saturday.

I could hear the dull noise of people leaving the fighting shed. Callie took up as master of ceremonies, cupping her voice as a hailer. I made out her shape in the cone of mist that angled from the streetlamp. People assembled around her as Hoofers did his thing. A din from the crowd ended in a groan as he jumped the car and they found they'd lost their money; I kept Unusual on the bit and was ready to do mine.

"And now," Callie announced, "just off the boat from Ireland, the horse who can jump cars." I saw Hoofers shifting people back from the roadside to make the going safe, clearing the takeoff and landing of roots and roughage like I'd told him.

"Lay your dollars down, three-to-one against a horse jumping this man as he lies along the hood," she said. Hoofers was in position, headlong on the hump, people dropping bills and coins; the bootleg and cockfight had whetted their taste for the bet.

"Cooee," Callie shouted like I'd taught her. I clucked Unusual forward from the trees and galloped down the sandy strip beside the road. His head bobbed with each stride towards the light, steam rose up from the snort of his breath, his hooves cupped out the sand along the track—fast enough for the effect but not so fast it got too dangerous. He needed to leave the ground about six feet out; too close he might clobber the car, turn turtle on the road. I hoped he wouldn't spook at Callie on the car roof, standing in the shadows like a scarecrow.

Hoofers appeared as a dark silhouette along the front of the car. He crowded his arms about his head. We took off a trifle long, but the horse was scopey and careful. We landed and galloped on free, down into the darkness.

I waited behind a hedgerow for the sound of the engine and the smiling getaway faces. We loaded him up in seconds and got back on the road before he'd barely broken a sweat.

"He could jump a house, that horse," said Hoofers.

"Then why you nearly pooed your pants?" Callie asked and we laughed.

"Eleven dollars and a half," he said; he'd already counted.

"All I could see was Hoofers' eyes, white as snowballs," I said as if I knew snow.

"We could go on to Trappe or Winslow, or down to Girdletree, do the same," said Hoofers.

"The horse is timber racing next weekend," I told him. "He's sort of stolen and the car's not exactly ours."

"We got clip-on Virginia licence plates," he said.

"A driver who's a foreigner, you're black, and I'm sixteen," said Callie, and that was pretty much that.

The windshield wipers scraped as we drove through drizzle. Hoofers fell quietly sideways, dozing with his face against the door. Callie was drowsy too; I was more awake than ever. I could have driven all night like that with those two, eleven dollars fifty in a hat in the glove box to be split three ways between us, Callie's head on my shoulder. She smelt like damp stacked hay, the sort that self-combusts and sets haystacks on fire, falling asleep with the corners of her mouth turned up. I wanted to kiss her more than anything. I wanted to say her name.

Callie hasn't appeared. From the hut I see Unusual picking at a biscuit of alfalfa in the field by the drive. He's been spelled for two months now; he bowed a tendon in the Virginia Gold Cup and still came third. I think of him galloping hurt, still trying. He won't race again. Tom Shackelton gave him to me.

I get up from my bed to go straighten his fly rug, though I know it'll only slip again. Something about the point of his croup and the angle to his hips makes it hard to keep his blanket in the middle. He stamps at a horsefly, turns to scratch his flank. I put my face against him for a moment, feel down his tendon.

I lie on the dry grass beside him like I did with my pony as a child. The familiar sound of a horse picking at grass nearby, the warm dry breath from his nose in my hair, sniffing me. His feet near my face but no danger. He wouldn't hurt me.

Callie wants him as a show jumper. She thinks he might be good enough to get her on the team and go to Europe. She wants to take him swimming. I said, "Hardly likely."

A truck rattles past but she still doesn't come. The sun sets over the forest, a mushroom above the trees. The warm air lies around me like a blanket; clouds of tummy-pink salmon. I close my eyes and listen to the road.

Callie and I leant up against the sides of a lawn jockey in front of the big house at Lower Wye—the first time we'd been alone together without Hoofers or horses. We'd known each other a week. Frogs jumped across the gravel driveway and disappeared into the dark. The grass was damp under our legs.

Her hand was freezing, she didn't feel the cold. We watched the lamplit shadow of the boss's wife sewing curtains in the attic, three storeys up the bricks and creeper. We waited for her to go to bed so we could have the run of the garden. The boss had gone to New York City.

"I left home when I was twelve," Callie said quietly. "They were after me for lighting fires."

"What kind of fires?"

"If you drag a dead branch burning through a dry grass field, it lights up behind you like a trail of turpentine."

"When I left home I rode so far I wore my pony's feet down," I said.

"Why'd you go?" she asked.

"My mother was dead." I looked up at the woman in the window, it reminded me of her. "I used to watch her sew at night, except she only had a kerosene lamp." She used sacks and flannel for curtains.

With Callie you don't have to pretend your family has money. "She had her things sent from Europe by boat, they came through the desert on the backs of camels, but most of them broke," I said.

"Her things or the camels?" asked Callie. I smiled but I didn't answer. I looked back up at the shape in the window. My mother would have loved it up there, sewing on a treadle machine, cutting slipcovers and curtains from English chintzes; helping the groundsman arrange the plantings for the seasons, training vines along the arbour trellis. Gardening gloves and secateurs, flowers growing wild beside the road.

"Last weekend I won the indoor puissance in Baltimore," Callie said. "They want me to join the U.S. team. They train at Boulderbrook."

"How high'd you jump?" I asked.

"Six four."

"I had a horse in Australia called Jinglebob," I told her. "We jumped six foot seven in the high jump at Wangaratta. Where's Boulderbrook?"

"New York."

The attic lamp went off and we waited for Shackelton's wife to turn off the downstairs lights and go to sleep. It felt good to stroke Callie's fingers. I didn't want her to leave.

"My father had a girlfriend. She lived on the place, but not in the house," I said.

"My mother was my father's girlfriend," said Callie. "They never bothered to marry."

When the house went dark the soft-lit swimming pool

water shone against the sky.

"Where's Hoofers?" I asked her.

"Tuesday Bible study," she said.

Callie went to the pool, she wanted to go in with no clothes on. In the raw, she called it. She shed her work jeans and shirt, dived in silently, the water hardly breaking. She swam down the length underneath, her arms by her sides, without coming up for breath. Up the other end she got out, not afraid of me seeing her. She nodded like I should do the same.

I dipped my fingers in. "The water's cold as Christmas," I whispered. Clouds ran high, lit by the moon. I didn't want her knowing I couldn't swim.

Callie stood pigeon-toed and hugged herself dripping. I took her clothes to her, she was tiny without them. I blew on her fingers to warm them, looked into her face and we kissed. Her hair was wet, her lips cold. As I closed my eyes I imagined her lighting fields on fire.

I wake in the field to the sound of a siren. Unusual has his head high up, sniffing the air. Callie never came to collect me. I sit up and smell burning. There's a fire in Tom Shackelton's field. Orange flames rope high in the darkness, the crackle of the ears as they catch, the cornstalks burn like broomstraw. From the bike I see the red light flashing through the trees. A crowd is gathering on Wye River Road.

"Deliberately lit. Started from the road," says Ricketts, the groundsman. Through the shapes of people watching I see Callie at the front, her face lit by flames. It seems odd that she'd be here alone. She didn't come to get me, Hoofers isn't with her.

I go over and stand beside her. She doesn't notice I'm there. Her body is contained but only just, the excitement of a child or dog about her. She stares into the fire like she sees the face of a secret friend.

"How come you didn't come over?" I ask her.

She doesn't turn to see me. "I came to watch the fire," she says.

"How did you know there was one?" I ask.

She doesn't answer. She catches a floating ember and holds it to her nose, it's almost as if she's smiling except she doesn't change her face.

Ricketts is watching who's about. He's walking over towards us.

"Is she with you?" he asks me. I nod, not looking at him, then realise he probably saw me riding down alone.

"She was on her way to visit me," I tell him. I wonder if he believes me, he isn't one to trust foreigners or people from out of state.

"The arsonist is usually among the onlookers," he says.

Callie doesn't seem impressed that I've protected her, it's like she knew I would. I want to search her for matches and a flask of kerosene. I watch her stare at the men in their overalls moving through the dark as they hose the remains, but she is not on their side. If people weren't here she'd stoke it. The flames no longer light her face, the firefighters have it under control. They wind in their hoses, trusting the dampness of night to keep the blackened field to a smoulder. People wander off to where they came from. Callie walks down towards Mrs. Voumard's car. I wonder if she'll ever like me more than lighting fires.

I gave my mother a cold-water cloth and she put it on her brow. I sat on the end of the bed. I was five years old. "When you were a baby there was a heat wave," she told me. She said the mercury in the thermometer that hung outside was stuck at the top. A hundred and twenty was as high as it went, but it was hotter than that, she said, each day for a month. "Dogs didn't come out from under the house." She put me in a wet hessian sack, laid me in the laundry basket on the corner of the porch. She hoped a breeze might come around the edge of the house but it didn't.

"There was nothing to breathe. I couldn't find air, not inside or out in the sun," she told me. She stood in the doorway and watched me. Dabbed my forehead with a wet washer, blew on my cheeks.

"You could have taken me away somewhere," I said. She didn't answer, that wasn't part of the story.

At night it was too hot to sew. She sat and she stood. She was afraid I might stop breathing. Other outback babies died in their cots. "Heatstroke exhaustion," she said. "You just looked up at the sky."

She thought I would die because I didn't blink. She couldn't remember whether babies were supposed to. There was no one to ask who would know.

She said she tried to sleep but mostly she didn't. She placed a bedroll on the veranda planks beside the basket where I lay. One night she dreamt a man was standing over her. A man she'd never seen.

My father couldn't bear her staring at me. "He told me I'd lost my shillings," she said. He began camping out by the billabong. She went down to bring him food. There were too many mosquitoes, she said, and it was the only place the kangaroos drank. They wouldn't come if he was there. "Bugger the kangaroos," he told her.

The milk from her body ran hot, she said, too hot for me to drink. She put it in bottles, buried them in the mud to cool when she went down at night to leave him food. A bottle exploded as she carried it back, she thought that she'd been shot.

When I survived she told my father it was because I was born on a boat. "That isn't logic," he said. She wondered if her mind hadn't been touched by the heat. "I never should have brought you here," she said. It was the end of her story.

"Why don't you take me away?" I asked her as I lay down on the bed beside her.

"Someone will come to take us away."

"Who?" I asked.

"You'll see," she said and went to sleep. I didn't sleep at all.

“We have to pick up Hoofers,” says Callie. I haven’t seen her since the fire. As we pass the burnt-out cornfield we both stare out into the blackness and go quiet.

At the end of the Wye River Road there’s a rustic hut set back in the trees. Tuesday night Bible study. Bethel African Methodist. We park the car around the corner like Hoofers asked us. It’s drizzling and dark. We’re fifteen minutes early.

“Let’s spy on him,” says Callie.

We scuttle through the woods, we don’t follow the road; we always go cross-country. I take cover under the eaves below a window where it’s mostly dry. The shrubs are damp around my feet and legs. Callie shoves in beside me. Through the louvres we see Hoofers standing with an open Bible in his hand. He has on a white stiff-collared shirt, starched, the top button done up. I’ve never seen him without his cap and dungarees. He’s reading out loud. In less than an hour he’ll be jumping cars for money.

“I didn’t know he was in charge,” I whisper.

Callie’s up on tiptoes, pushing me so she can see. But the window is closed, we can’t hear.

By the time we get to the door, someone’s playing the piano, making enough noise that they don’t hear us crawl in. We kneel behind some free-standing chairs at the back.

An old woman with her hair in a bun sits a few rows ahead, the others are all up near the front.

A pale-faced Jesus hangs on the wall, askew, as if the cross is falling sideways. Hoofers starts singing a song. His voice is surprising, much lower than when he talks. I can hear the words clearly, but I don't understand what they mean. "There is a balm in Gilead," he says. At first I think he says "a bomb."

He has a grey streak in his hair where his pigment is pale, it makes him look older than he is. He's in his twenties, older than Callie and me. When he finishes singing, the people keep humming.

"Close your eyes and pick yourself a scripture," he says to a man in the front with hair shellacked across his head.

"Chronicles," says the man, "11:12," his voice from way back in his head.

"After Jashobeam was Eleazar the son of Dodo," reads Hoofers.

I don't think it's one he's heard of. He wrestles the air to come up with a meaning. He doesn't know what he's doing. "It's about sons and fathers," he says. "What's your father's name?"

"Never knew his name," the old man says. Hoofers reads on, looking for something else. Then it comes to him.

"Your father's name is God," says Hoofers.

"My father's name is Darwin," I whisper to Callie. She thinks it's funny and snorts. The woman in front of us half looks around, but she's too fat to make the turn. Her movement catches Hoofer's eye; he sees us in the back. He doesn't wink or smile, just shakes his head like we shouldn't be seen.

Callie stands up and points to her watch. It's already time to be on the road. She doesn't want to miss the cockfight. We have thirty miles to drive, but Hoofers isn't finished.

"Let me speak from Judges," he says, thumbing pages. I've never heard of Judges; the Bible isn't something I've read.

"And Samson caught three foxes, and set them afire." Hoofers looks right at us, I can tell he's talking to Callie. "He let them go unto the sturdy corn, and burnt up both the shocks and also the sturdy corn and all the field around," he says.

The woman in front of us can tell Hoofers speaks past her. She turns herself around this time and looks at Callie. Her eyes are deep set and simmering. It's the mother of the boy who's under suspicion for lighting the field. A boy called Seaweed.

Callie is gone from beside me, she runs through the rain to the car. I follow her out. She drives without talking, the wipers scrape the glass. The high beams from an oncoming truck light her face, she is fierce with concentration. I've never seen her this angry before, more than when the horse drowned.

She stops on the roadside where she picked me up and waits for me to get out. We're not going to Girdletree.

"It was just a fucking cornfield," she says and drives away.

Except for the flies, it was silent; there was no breeze. The sun bit my scalp. I was six years old and the billabong was full. We didn't know why, it hadn't rained for years.

I leant on a stick like an old man and waited for my mother to catch up. My arms were tanned up to my elbows, the rest of me was pale as she was.

Every day I'd asked her if she'd teach me to swim but she didn't like to leave the garden. Then she started sewing something. She made me a pair of baggy trunks that hung from the narrow of my hips.

The towel was pulled around my shoulders, I nuzzled in close to her as we walked. Her white-skirted bathers brushed against my arm. She carried a towel of her own and a special rubber cap. She'd been swimming before, but that was in Europe.

She moved her sun umbrella to an angle that shaded me and looked down at my feet. They were dusty and bare as always, the colour of the sand.

"I wish you would wear shoes," she said. I didn't like them, they blistered the tops of my toes. She had on lace-up boots with heels. I trod carefully to avoid the bindi burrs and tiny sharp remnants of shells in the sand. The sand that now bore poisonous snakes; I'd seen them hanging dead on fences.

My mother was swollen with a baby. It pulled the material at her waist, made her bathers look uncomfortable. She brought it with her from Vienna. She said they don't have snakes there.

We put our towels and the umbrella down at the base of the coolibah tree. There was a streak of shade, the width of the trunk, that stretched out over the water.

"It's like a beach of our own," she said, "three hundred miles from the sea."

Fresh water had seeped up from an eye in the earth below the reeds and spilt out over the sand like a tongue of honey. I knelt on all fours at the edge, I was a wallaby drinking. It was cool on my lips, not brackish or salty, but pure as water running in a river. But it didn't move, it was still like glass. A stone I threw went plonk in the middle where the bottom was dark. The red, scented lilies wobbled on their pads and the ripples they made lapped the edge where I waited.

"You can go in," she told me. "He said it's safe."

My father said he'd thrown in a cattle dog to make sure there weren't any crocodiles, but you didn't get crocodiles that far south. He said things like that to make her scared. That's why she hardly left the house.

The water came up to my chest, it felt warm like hands around me. Clear-winged insects stood weightless on the surface, my face just inches from them. The light reflected like rainbows on the film of their wings. I stroked the air with my hand and they flew lazily away, making sounds like purring cats.

My mother sat down in the shallow behind me, cooling herself. “I’ll teach you to swim,” she said.

She was sweeping her arms under the surface to show me how to move my legs without splashing. “Like frogs do,” she said. She held my hands firmly as I kicked and it made my head sway back and forth. The sun shone on the ripples.

I looked up at her as she blew at a strand of her hair. It fell from her cap, her fingers not free to tuck it. Still holding my hands, she walked me in deeper where there was mud underfoot. The water came over the swell of her belly, the skirt of her bathers was floating.

“Put your head under this time and open your eyes in the water,” she told me.

I took a breath and blew out my cheeks, floated face down. The sound of water filled my ears. I could see to the bottom, the stirrings in the mud about her feet. Swimming is easy, I thought. The reeds wandered around her legs, her skirt billowed, and then there was blood; it ran from her thinly, scribbled in the water like ink. Her body jerked sideways. She bent at the knees and let go of my hands. I shut my eyes and floundered, took in a mouthful of water, swung my arms until there was sand under my knees and it was shallow. I didn’t know what was happening.

She squatted in the water and struggled from her bathers. Blood came up in her hands.

“What is it?” I asked her. She didn’t speak. She pulled off her plastic swim cap and put what had happened inside it. Her hair unfolded and fell down over her face; she wiped it back with her hands still full, a smear of red against her brow. I gave her the towel but she motioned me away.

She crouched at the edge of the water and scooped a hole, covered the cap and what was in it with sand. She looked anxiously at the ground. I knew it wouldn't have happened if I hadn't kept asking to swim, if she'd stayed in the house. She got up and moved past me like a blind woman, her hands all over her face. She hadn't wanted to come. I picked up the towel and umbrella, her bathers, and her boots. The cattle dogs came down the track and barked at her.

She stopped and turned, as if she'd forgotten I was with her. She looked older than before. She didn't put her boots back on.

"We shouldn't have come to the water," I said. She took her bathers from me and hugged them to her stomach. She didn't say it wasn't my fault.

My underarms feel tight in the early morning cold. I crouch in the wet and wait for Callie, behind a clump of birch so the horse can't see me. I close my hand around the damp bamboo. She's been strange since the fire.

In Maryland the woods are everywhere, sometimes it feels too close. At first I liked being where it was thick with foliage, but there are times I miss dry air and wide expanses. I didn't grow up in the mud.

Callie canters down the track towards me; I hear the familiar rhythm of Unusual's stride. I check the bamboo pole, make sure the horse won't see it. I catch a narrow glimpse of them between the ashy trunks. Callie sits up on him coolly, she's done this before. It's the horse who's unsuspecting.

They leave the ground and jump the log pile beside me. I swing the pole and clout the horse in his open shins, in the place we shaved with clippers and rubbed with turpentine. I hit him strong the first time, on his cannon bones, just the way she told me. The whacking of it echoes through the trees and up between my fingers. I've caught him unawares.

The horse makes a grunt as he lands; the sound sits uneasily around me as I watch them lope away. He's already trying his hardest. It's just a sting, a bit of bruising, but I know by the way my underarms ache that I don't like it. She calls it "preparing him" so he won't touch the jumps. "Making a good horse special," she says. I know that there are things I'll do for Callie if she asks me.

There's a breaking of twigs in the woods behind me, another horse through the trees.

"I think someone saw us," I say to Callie as we head back to the show ground. She doesn't get down from the horse.

"People get sneaky before the Grand Prix," she says. I can't tell if she's talking about us or them.

I smooth out the groove where the pole met his hair, check his old bowed tendon. You wouldn't notice it if you weren't looking.

"I didn't like doing it," I say.

"He's just a horse," she says.

The way she dismisses it makes me sad. We walk back to the show barns in silence, keeping our thoughts to ourselves. It's more important for her to win, that's the difference between us. She can be cruel without being angry.

Unusual's breath puffs in front of him, steam from the sweat on his neck. His eyes are kind, big like a seal's. I rub him with a towel as I walk alongside, a creamy line of lather where the breastplate goes. I say a silent "sorry" as I wipe it. I don't want her riding him.

"Why didn't you get Hoofers to help you?" I ask.

"He wouldn't do it," she says. She pulls some leaves from an overhead branch. I put my hand on her jodhpur leg, reach my fingers around her calf, the tops of her paddock boots. The rib of her sock, a touch of her skin.

"Have you ever loved anyone?" I ask her. I close my fingers firmly around her ankle as we walk; my middle finger almost touches my thumb.

"You're the only one I can trust," she says. I look up at the greens in the trees and for a moment I close my eyes.

"I'd rather be loved than trusted," I say.

On Fridays, Shackelton's wife, Rosemary, storms the garden, a glass of red wine in one hand and a cigarette ringed with lipstick in the other. One time in June she had me help her, cutting stems of flowers in bloom: roses, lilacs, and narcissus. She was most enthusiastic, teaching me their names. Dahlias, daphnes, daffodils. She arranged them with Queen Anne's lace in lavish painted vases, had me place them up on tables and antique pedestals around the downstairs rooms, ready for when she'd pick her husband up from the train. She said she liked listening to my accent.

"How old are you?" she asked me in the garden, her cashmered breast against my forearm as she leant to smell the lilacs. I wasn't sure if I should move or stay to meet the brush of her body.

"Eighteen," I told her. Her scent was of perfumes and powder, smoke.

"Cut me some of those," she said. "Their season is so short, I hate to see them go." She was either from England or sounded like it. She had corn-blond hair, not unlike my mother's. Her laugh rang around me like an echo. I was nervous with her on my own, the way she was with the boss not around.

"I'm thirty-six," she said.

I acted like I was surprised.

"Don't we have enough flowers?" I asked her.

"Yairs," she said, mimicking the way I talked.

"I don't sound like that," I said.

She took a sip from her glass, added to the lipstick prints. "You and that little Calliope Coates. Running around the garden like farts in a bath. Probably has you prowling 'round the county with that negro groom of hers." I wondered if she'd seen Callie naked by the pool.

"She's got tickets on herself. Funny little thing. Feet so small she's plucky to be out on them. Ankles you could snap with your hands."

"Callie's good enough to go to the Olympics," I told her. "I have tickets on her too."

Callie and I lay together with our clothes on, up in the cockloft. I didn't tell her what Rosemary Shackelton said. I wanted to take her to my hut but she preferred being up high with the view.

We looked out from under the peak of the barn along the long gravel drive, over broodmares and foals in the front field, the manicured forest. We watched Tom Shackelton walk down from the house, our elbows in the hay.

"Skinny," said Callie. She hadn't seen him before.

He wore abridgement breeches, braces and lace-up shoes, a deerstalker's hat. "He thinks it's 1860," I said. He headed past the dovecote to the kennel, where the fox-hounds whined. He'd imported two pups from the Duke of Norfolk's pack in England, he took them out for runs. He called them Benson and Hedges.

"He's old as God," said Callie as he got closer.

Rosemary, not one for walking, followed him down in the wood-sided station wagon and parked. She just came to observe.

"I love watching when they don't know I'm here," I said. I felt Callie's skin underneath her windcheater; she muffled a laugh as she pushed me away.

"Your hands are frozen," she whispered. She always says that when I touch under her clothes. I knew my hands were warm and my blood was pumping. It's my feet that are always cold. I wanted to feel her skin so badly.

Shackelton let the pups out and they followed their noses along the ground, straight into the barn below us. We could hear them whine and scratch the slats on the ladder up the wall.

"Bugger off," I hissed under my breath.

The car door closed as Rosemary came over to make sure they weren't in trouble. She knew the old man couldn't keep up if they ran astray.

"What's up there, pups?" she said from below. She always talks to animals.

"Have a look, will you, Buddie-Boo?" said Shackelton. I didn't know he called her that. Callie opened her mouth in a silent scream of laughter at the name. There was nowhere to hide. We could have jumped outside, it was a drop we could handle, but they'd hear us and the dogs would follow. Rosemary Shackelton peered above the level of the loft and saw us. Callie and I sat separate.

"Just a couple of stray cats in the hay," she said. She raised her eyes and smiled like she had one on us.

"I think we should burn this barn and build a new one," she said as she got back down. "On Guy Fawkes night, like they do in London. Have a party and raze the lot of it."

They coaxed the pups outside. We could hear them on the gravel.

"She saw us in the garden by the pool," I told Callie.

"How do you know?"

"She told me. She had me cut flowers for the house."

Callie got quiet like I'd joined the other side. I wished I hadn't mentioned it. "I was just cutting flowers. Why won't you let me touch you?"

"You do it too rough," she said.

I looked at my hands, they were dry and bumped. They could have been my father's.

"I don't like men's hands," she said.

"Then you touch *me*," I said.

Her fingers were cold and steady, they traced the shapes in my face. It wasn't all that I wanted, but it was more than enough.

It's five miles to Presqu'Ile, the farm where Callie works. The wheels of my bike creak faster than usual. She's leaving for Boulderbrook, to train with the U.S. team. She didn't tell me herself, I heard it elsewhere. We haven't spoken since I took Unusual back.

A low-lying fog scarfs the dips in the Trappe Road. I can't really see where I'm going: I get off the tarmac when car lights come. It must be almost midnight, I forgot to wind my watch.

The road to the mouth of the Choptank runs straight into the driveway. Callie has a bungalow near the barn. I haven't been inside it, I've only seen it from the road. She's never invited me in.

There's a light on at the stable, but the horses are gone from the stalls. I dump the bike in the hedge where it won't be seen. Callie's door is slightly open, the room looks empty. Maybe she left on the lorry, travelled with the horses. I feel for the switch on the wall, but there isn't one, so I pull the drapes to let in the light from the barn. The wardrobe is open but there's nothing inside it. The bed is in the corner, in the shadows. Callie's lying on it, her hands are behind her head.

"What are you doing?" I say, as though she's the one who's broken in.

"Waiting till morning," she says.

She wears a knitted cardigan and tartan pants. Her good pants. She doesn't seem surprised that I'm there.

"How did you know it was me?" I ask. I walk around the room as if I'm looking for something.

"You have a loud bike," she says.

I don't know whether to sit or stand. It's stuffy, so I open the window. The air makes the hangers tinkle in the cupboard.

"Your room has nothing in it," I say. I wish I'd seen it with her things. I sit on the end of the bed. The mattress is bare and uneven, no blankets or sheet.

"Everything went with the horses," she says.

"How come you didn't tell me you were leaving?"

"I thought it would be better if I was just gone."

On the wall beside the bed there are jumping pictures, plastered from horse magazines and books she shared with me before she cut them up. She's made a sort of collage. At the edge there's a small black-and-white photo. It's me on Jinglebob at Wangaratta, a picture I gave her from *Hoofs and Horns*. I reach over and unpaste it, slowly so it doesn't rip. I fold it in half.

"Here, take me with you," I say. I put it in the pocket of her pants. "I might not be in a magazine again."

"You'll never be as famous as me," she says. "You're not as hard on horses."

I lie down on the bed beside her. The ceiling slants low above our heads, the rain has made patches of damp in the plaster like imaginary countries.

"When I sleep on my back I have nightmares," I say.

She turns on her side and faces me. Her knitted cardigan smells of straw, it has some seeds from feeding hay. I pull a prickle from the wool.

"I thought you had already left," I say.

"I don't like driving in the dark," she says. Her hands are cold, I rub them. She usually tells me the truth.

"Did you know I would come?" I ask.

I unbutton her cardigan deliberately, she neither helps nor hinders me. She has nothing on underneath it, the scratchy wool against her skin. I trace my fingers on her stomach, slowly making shapes. She looks into the darkness where the rafters meet the floor. She doesn't answer my question.

I lean over and kiss her, softly like I don't mean more. She touches my hair, her fingers more certain than when they're on my skin.

"Can't we just stay here?" I ask.

She looks out of the window, as if there's something to be seen. There's just the black night sky, the glare of the light outside.

Her eyes tighten as I move to lie on top of her. For a moment I lie still, my hands along the bottom of her back. Her skin is soft and cool, her mouth slightly open. The feel of me against her makes her shudder slightly, a quick breath in her throat. She moves out from under me.

"What's wrong?" I ask, reaching to her.

She starts to say something but doesn't. She shakes her head in a way that makes her look older.

"Can't," she says. She stands and buttons her cardigan, flattens the front of her pants. "You can stay here if you like," she says.

"Will you take me back in the morning? We can put the bike in the car."

"I won't be here in the morning," she says.

She goes outside as if to get some air, but keeps on walking through the trees to the car. I get up and follow, call out after her, but her head is low, she doesn't look back. The car door closes in the dark, then the lights come on and she drives away. The back seat brims with luggage.

I stand barefoot in the cold, dark branches, my breath out in front of me, and watch the car fade into the fog. I know that I am sorry, I just don't know what for.

I'd heard grown-ups talk of the flood bird but I'd never seen one before. I was nine years old. A line of water peeled slowly across the desert towards my mother and me; it came from a far-off rain. The day was so clear you wouldn't think flood. The sun burned a white hole in the sky. My father wasn't home.

I stood on the roof of the house with my mother, my hand in hers. My hat had a brim that flopped. The bird circled the house making low-pitched sounds. "Can you see the waters?" my mother said, pointing into the haze. She held my hand tightly as I squinted into the sun. The water came shiny and gradual, like a silver sheet unravelling.

We'd put things up high, prepared the house. Chairs on tables, foodstuffs and photos above the Coolgardie safe. My shirts on top of the wardrobe.

We pulled the ladder up in case it washed away, then ate our bread and Vegemite from a wooden board. I could tell my mother wasn't hungry, she only ate so I would.

The silence was odd. No sign of the men on horses. My father was out on the muster with Dickie Del Mar. Dickie was the cattleman, he came from Argentina. He wore a broad straw hat, knotted tight under his chin. My father called him Dickie. His real name was Alphonse.

"Father says Dickie's hat looks stupid with a chin

strap," I told her.

"Your father's hat falls off each time he canters," she said.

Distant anthills, higher than I was, collapsed at their bases as the water crept past. Meat ants collected around us on the rotting timber halves we sat on. I wondered if they somehow knew to get up high or if they were just attracted by the bread.

I spent a lot of time with Dickie but we didn't talk that much. I liked to watch him with the horses. He was a proper horseman, played polo in Buenos Aires before he went to Europe. My father named him Dickie the day he arrived with a hundred longhorn steers. He'd met up with a cattle drive coming south from way up past the Diamantina.

"Dickie's teaching me how to plait leather, cut with a knife. He's making a homemade bridle," I told my mother.

From the roof we could see the river in the distance, the line of the trees now bathed in a low, silent ocean. As night fell around us, she held on to my shoulder, her fingers digging in. She mumbled under her breath. I wondered if she was praying.

We watched the water come halfway up the garden, quietly like a timid visitor, then stop about twelve feet out. For half an hour we stood and watched it lap the roots of the Moreton Bay fig. The darkness filled with mosquitoes. The night air came in cold. The stars seemed closer than usual.

My mother lit the paraffin lamp. I sat down on the roof and hugged my knees. Her pale arms were bare and folded. She wouldn't sit. She didn't have a pullover. The long lace dress she'd made from a tablecloth hung in shadows from her shoulders. She'd become thin, not enough skin to cover her bones. Her colour in the lamplight was almost clear. The purple of her veins showed through on her forehead and neck, her cheeks were hollow. Insects swarmed around her, drawn by the flame. She used to sing to crowds.

"I don't understand why you wait up for Father," I told her.

"It's not just him," she said.

I closed my eyes and listened. Tiny black figs plopped softly from the tree into the water below, the sizzle of insects on the lamp. There was no sign of men on horses sloshing through the wet.

My mother and Dickie, they talked a lot. He knew a lot of languages, but his English wasn't good. They spoke French together. She called him Alphonse.

The water wasn't moving closer. "Let's get down and go to bed," I said. She let her hair loose but didn't braid it. "Can I sleep in your room?" I asked.

"Your father says nine is too old to sleep with your mother."

"But he's not here," I said.

She held me to her, put her face against my hair, her arms around my waist. She warmed her body on mine. Her fingers were so cold they sent a shiver through my back. A dampness had risen from the water to her skin, she smelt like the flood. I could feel her breasts against me. I wondered if she'd have rather been with Dickie or if she was happy it was me.

I woke to the sound of my mother grunting. It was morning. I sat up and watched her through the window. She never came to bed.

She turned shovels of soil in the wet half of the garden, transferred a dying bush to where the ground was muddy, moved a barrowload of clay to where the flood water hadn't come.

My father walked in alone on a hot and tired horse. Dickie Del Mar wasn't with him. He wanted tea and hot water and didn't want to talk to her. My mother kept on digging while I got out of bed and dressed.

I stayed out of his way, went outside and hoed the garden with Mother; we worked the wet soil. The flood came no further, it had been soaked up. The sand we turned was a bright, wet orange.

The fly-wire door squealed and banged shut. I looked up at my father. "Get the pony," he told me. "I want Day to see the river," he said to my mother. He didn't usually call me by name.

"Where's Alphonse?" she asked.

"He was too afraid to cross."

I didn't look at her. I went out with my father, bareback so I didn't need shoes. I could keep up with him without a saddle, I used a sack instead.

The desert had bloomed overnight with meadows of tiny purple flowers like furry carpets; their seeds must have waited for years in the sand. A flock of dark swans flew so low overhead their shadows quivered over us, spooking my father's horse. He called his horse Boss Hog, said he was unreliable.

The Murrumbidgee had overshot its banks, it was half a mile wide, fat as a lake. It had taken out the bridge. From the edge he pointed to a shadow up a tree out in the middle. It looked like a rangy cow stuck high in a branch, something dragging in the water out ahead of it. It was strange to see a dead thing so high up.

"What is it?" I asked.

He kicked the horse into the water where the current wasn't strong and I followed so we could get closer. It was Dickie Del Mar.

"Never swim on a horse across a flooding river," my father said, waving flies from his face with a stick. "You have to send your horse ahead of you and grab on to its tail, get dragged across behind." He pointed at Dickie's body. "I told him but he didn't listen."

The horse was wedged in a fork of a river gum, and he was strung up in front of it. The reins were caught around his neck, his legs were out ahead of him in the drag of the water. Ravens hovered over him. One settled on his shoulder, another on his hat.

My pony stamped in the water, ready to head for home. I didn't want to look but I couldn't stop.

It was Dickie who carried me on his shoulders, let me

steer him around the stockyards by the handlebars of his moustache, my thighs around his neck. He taught me to tango in the garden, my bare feet on the zip up the middle of his boots, clinging around his waist. Dipping and bowing through the sheets and pillowcases, my face in the sweat on his chest where the buttons of his shirt stayed open, my mother laughing, hanging his clothes on the line.

At lunch he would sit beside her when my father had already eaten and gone. Lying on the ground underneath the table I looked at the hairs on his legs as they talked. Once I almost held my face against his ankle. He pretended I wasn't there. Sometimes my mother's leg would brush against his and stay there. After he arrived, she stopped wearing socks, put a ribbon in her hair.

But he was out on the water, hanging from his horse, his hat still strapped to his head. I felt dizzy like I did when I had a concussion.

My father turned his horse, rough with his hands, and rode for home. In the Backblock Paddock I jumped off the pony beside a patch of kangaroo paw that had blossomed among the paddymelons in the flood. I picked a cluster of the fire-orange flowers. I would give them to my mother.

When I caught up with my father, he took the flowers from me. As we reached the house, he leant down and gave the flowers to my mother in the yard.

"These are from Dickie," he said. She looked at the ground. She must have thought that Dickie had left her. I didn't tell her he was dead. He was supposed to take us away.

I get off the train in New York City. I haven't seen Callie since October. I don't like the look of it as I walk out on Seventh Avenue, but I'm glad the streets are numbered. It's Nations' Cup night at Madison Square Garden, her first time on the team. Thirty-seven days since she left me in the dark at Presqu'Ile.

The horse show is on top of the railway station, seven storeys up. Ticketholders only are allowed to get there in the lift. I didn't even have a ticket for the train.

I go around the back of the building, sneak up the ramp with a horse being led up to the stables, as if I am one of the grooms, then I watch from the collecting ring, among the potted plants and filler. A swing band plays show tunes, women wearing gloves sit just near me. I spit on my fingers to fix my hair.

Callie has one fence down, no one's yet gone clear. She rides from the arena, serious like a little girl, goes right by me as if I'm not there. I want to go to her but Buddy Black appears. I've seen his photo in the magazines. He hugs her hard, it's more than congratulations. I stand there like a shrub.

I follow them back to the stable area: Callie, the horse, and her hangers-on. I wait nearby, standing in the aisle. Callie sits down on a bale of hay, Buddy Black pulls off her boots. She can't ignore me, I'm right there.

"What are you doing here?" she asks, an unlikely shrillness in her voice.

"I came up on the train," I say.

"This is Day," she announces. "He's Australian," she says, like it's an excuse.

"G'day Day," says one of them, as though they were the first to ever have said it. Buddy Black looks at me.

"Can I talk with you?" I ask Callie.

She looks inconvenienced, leads me around the corner and into an empty stall.

"Are you with him now?"

She doesn't answer, looks away.

"You're supposed to be with me."

"I'm not supposed to be with anyone," she says.

"Why did you run away?" I hold her shoulders. I want to shake her, but I just hold them. She reaches her hand and rubs behind her neck. Drops of rain start banging on the roof.

"I was leaving anyway," she says.

"But we're best friends."

"You wanted me to do things," she says.

"And you light fires," I say. It's the first time she looks at me. "And you're with Buddy now."

"Fuck Buddy Black," she says.

I pull her to me, try to kiss her face, but she turns and frees her mouth, calls out to the others as if she's needing help. I hear them coming, the famous Buddy Black. He comes in and puts his arm around her.

“Everything okay, Callie?” he asks. He’s so American.

“Her name’s Calliope,” I say. He looks at me oddly.

The others stand there, waiting for me to leave. They think that I’m a danger.

At first I walk and then I’m running, through the stables and down the ramps and into the street, into the hot dirty rain; I look back in case Callie is coming. But she’s not, he must be holding on to her.

I close the doors behind me on the train back to Baltimore, sit down in the corner. I watch myself in the window, like I’ve done on trains before, my wet face reflected in the glass.

It is summer, 1956, more than six months later. Tom Shackelton's men are cutting hay in big round bales I haven't seen before. On weekdays I go riding with Rosemary if he's out of town. She has a horse called History who's a good field hunter. She rides sidesaddle, sometimes astride. She doesn't like to ride alone. I ride Unusual.

"History's a thoroughbred," she reminds me, even though he obviously isn't. He looks crossbred to me, like one of his forebears pulled a plough.

We follow paths along the Wye. It's so green I have hay fever. I try not to sniff or think about Callie.

"Callie Coates is gone," she says. I nod like I don't care, looking up above me, the clouds so high they don't leave shadows. "I heard she got caught rapping a horse with bamboo, six months' suspension, she's not on the team." I pretend I already know.

"My bottom's feeling fragile," she says. "Let's get off and walk."

I know what she's up to. Ever since I came, when she looked at me and didn't introduce herself, I knew one day that this could happen if I stayed around.

She ties History to a sapling on a wooded rise, I hitch Unusual to a birch. As she pulls her scarf from around her chin, her hair falls down about her shoulders. Her hair is fair; when I touch it, it is not unlike my mother's.

The scarf has a fox-hunting scene across it, unfolds to the size of a picnic blanket. The grass pokes up at it as she places it on the ground. A tiger butterfly plays in the air. I don't really want to kiss her, even though she looks pretty, I just hold my face against her head. The smell of perfume and powder. The horses stamp at botflies and nibble at trees as I press against her into the silk. Underneath her half-bloused shoulder, hounds are running down a fox in the field in the pattern of the scarf. I close my eyes and think of Callie. I have a dry taste in my mouth; it's not how I'd imagined it would be.

I walk through the trees to the field where the racetrack is. Cars are parked all over. Culpeper is hot this time of year. The race is called the Virginia Honeysuckle; they say it's supposed to be dangerous. There's a boy leant up against a clapped-out truck.

"White people usually don't come here," he says.

I catch sight of Callie. She's wearing green silks, being bunked up on a swishy-tailed mare. My stomach gets tight when I see her. I get in the shade of a rickety stand of bleachers, in the back so I'm hidden. I've been following her too long.

"Are you with the white girl?" the boy asks. I nod as if I still am. There are no other white people here.

Girls in dresses sell beer from a long trestle table. Some of the men aren't walking straight, some lean up on others, mostly they don't notice me.

"We call her Snow White," says the boy.

A man lies out on the ground, half beneath the bleachers. He looks like he's been stabbed with a bottle but no one seems concerned. Horses and jockeys mill around, down one end where a man stands on a chair. The jockeys seem bigger than usual, or maybe the horses are smaller. Some of them are starey coated, some of them aren't that bad. Callie's riding short, her knees up around her chin.

I want to be out there with her.

Callie's been riding races since she got rubbed out from horse shows, but she can't ride at real racecourses, like Pimlico and Belmont—only men are allowed. She always said one day she'd get a licence, be the first woman jockey. Meanwhile she races at places like this. On my days off I watch her.

A loose horse gallops past, dragging the post it was tied to. It heads through the crush at the starting line. Horses and riders run sideways and some of the jockeys get off. You can't see much for the dust. Callie stays on board. Her mare is snaky, pinning its ears at the others.

The gun goes off while some of the riders are barely back on, others face the wrong way. Callie breaks out running at the front end. She has racing goggles, the only one who does. But she doesn't need them, she stays ahead of the dust. Some of the riders are left so far behind they give the whole thing up. A man throws a brick at the starter.

The track is narrow, with roots on the surface and only an inside rail. I recognise Callie's mare as she passes, low in the middle and high at the ends. She named her "Miss Furs"; her winter coat came out in big patches. I remember when she got her. "Like riding a soup sandwich," she said. You wouldn't run a good horse here.

The race becomes a cloud of dust along the back of the field, it passes a clapboard house. I can only see bits and pieces. People begin to crowd forward, pushing up into the stand. Some of them get up on planks between barrels. A man drops his drink and says, "Jesus."

The horses storm back along the rail, into the rough-stubble stretch. I watch for Callie. I'm the one not shouting. She's still out in front, she whips the most consistently, each time in the exact same place. "Beating the moths from the sofa," she calls it.

The boy beside me cranes his neck to see. "She'd make a box spring gallop," I say, but he doesn't know what I'm talking about.

People drunk with the dust and the beer and the afternoon sun get to their feet and roar with the others who are already standing. Callie wins easily with two lengths to spare. She rides past the prize-giving and straight towards the makeshift grandstand where I hide. She knows she's not supposed to, but she avoids presentations and ceremonies.

Men and women rattle down the planks to pat the winner and see the white girl close up. Callie jerks the mare in the mouth so she doesn't bite their outstretched hands. I stay underneath, among the empty cans and bottles, beside the man who's bleeding and another who's fallen down drunk. "Be careful, her horse could kick," I say to the boy. He looks at me suspiciously.

"If you know her so well, why don't you go over yourself?" he says.

I get glimpses of Callie through the boards and pant legs. I don't think she sees me. She takes off her goggles and smiles as she talks to each of them; she doesn't mind if they're drunk. She likes it here. She's having more fun than the other times I've watched her lately.

One by one the people go back to their drinking, the

boy disappears. Callie gets down from the horse and takes off the saddle. No one seems to weigh in or out. Her new groom comes over and takes Miss Furs. He's already collected the trophy, a cheap beer mug, and a red rosette. Callie jokes with him like he's her brother, holding his forearm as she talks, the way she used to with Hoofers.

I follow them back to the trailer but I stay in the cover of trees. I know what she's saying even though I can't hear. How friendly the people are, how useless the mare is, how she got out first and stayed there. Her hair is standing up and matted from the racing cap. She runs her fingers through it. She didn't used to care about appearances. I remember how we'd return to the stables at horse shows, how I'd pull off her boot and the sock would come with it. I'd tickle her feet and we'd fall to the ground. It feels good being near her, even if she doesn't know.

Hoofers is waiting with the car and trailer as though he hasn't bothered to watch. I didn't expect him here, didn't know they were still friends. Callie gets in the front seat with him. I lean up against a tree and watch them as the light fades down around me and shines along the car. They sit until the sky turns purple. I want to go over but I don't. They laugh and then she kisses him. She puts her face about his cheeks and neck, and then against his mouth. He's dark against her skin, awkward like they've not done it before. It catches my chest and takes the breath from me. I slide down the bark and sit in the dirt, then I get up and I'm walking over to them. I don't care if they see me.

Hoofers rolls down the window and they look at me

like they knew I was coming. "'Bout time you came out of the trees," says Callie. She turns and sits sideways to face me. Hoofers won't look, he knows how I feel. He was my friend too. I look at the ground, there's a bottle in the dirt. I want to pick it up and break it on something.

"You shouldn't have done that," I say.

"What?" asks Callie.

"Kiss."

"We knew you were there," she says, "Your face as white as paint." I don't like the way she dismisses it.

"It wasn't fair," I say. My voice is brittle, it quavers, my disappointment doesn't sound good. I wanted to be more resolute.

"You can't keep following her around," says Hoofers. "It only makes things worse."

"Are you still with Buddy Black?" I ask her. I know he travels the horse shows.

"You know that's not it," she says. She looks at Hoofers like he's supposed to say something.

"I'll have more chance on my own," she says.

"I thought we'd do that stuff together," I say.

"We can't both be women jockeys," she says.

I stamp the bottle into the dirt, it makes a hollow sound but doesn't break. The leaves are noisy under my feet, my breathing is loud and deliberate, everything is amplified.

"I'm sorry," says Callie. She reaches past Hoofers and out the window, with a piece of paper in her hand.

"What's that?" I ask her.

"My address if you want to write."

I take the paper and read it. Her writing is scratchy, not like mine. I fold it in half and put it in the pocket of my pants. "I shouldn't have come to America," I say.

The name on the gate says THE EASTERBROOKS. I lean forward and look through the windshield wipers: horses with canvas blankets in fields around a big wooden house shielded by oaks and chestnut trees. I take the address out of my pocket. I know it by heart: c/o Easterbrook, Monkton, Maryland. I've read it fifteen times.

Callie's old plastic rain scarf lies on the driveway. I pick it up and tie it to the side mirror of her white Studebaker. I hear talking inside the house, the kitchen window is open. A man's voice that isn't Hoofers's; it doesn't have the drawl of the Eastern Shore. It's Buddy Black. He looks short without his riding boots on. He takes a can of Fanta from the fridge and goes into another room. I move along the windows.

They sit on the bed and leaf through Callie's scrapbook. On the wall above them there's a painting of an old woman in a long dress, leading a peacock in a harness. Buddy sits close to Callie as she turns the pages and talks. I stand in a ficus not ten feet from them, but I can't hear what they say.

She points at pictures—I know most of them even though I can't see. I remember how each of them sits on the page. Callie at horse shows and local gymkhanas when she was younger, cuttings of point-to-points and cross-country races. Some I took myself with her Box Brownie: Hoofers jumping the car, Callie on a horse on the Delaware beach. One of me on Untouchable over a sunken road.

Callie looks young on the bed, even with her face full of shadows. Buddy is older, he must be twenty-seven or -eight. He closes the book and leans back, pulls her down beside him. She looks straight up at the ceiling as if she can see right through the roof.

I move from the window, not afraid of the noise I make, the swing of a branch that slaps the glass, the sound of my feet on the gravel. I hear them get up from the bed but I don't look around. I get in the car and slam the door, drive fast along the narrow roads, follow the signs to Baltimore.

I think about my mother. The way she'd shed her shoe and brush my calf with her unstockinged foot. A quiet back-and-forthing under the dining room table. The nights alone she strained her eyes in the light of the slush lamp while I stood quiet in the dirt outside, after my bedtime, watching her through the crack between flour sacks she'd nailed up as drapes. The blue cambric dress she gathered and seamed from curtains. Prettied with lace at the waist, wrists, and hem, red flowers sewn all over.

The punkah hung from the ceiling of my mother's sewing room, framed like a makeshift sail. During the day, I sat at her feet and pulled the plaited cord in a rhythm to swing the silk-filled border; each swath it made across the room brought a breeze to cool her. She wrestled the cloth in the one-cushioned chair.

When the outfit was finished, buttoned with roses, she stood in it shyly, ready to go into town, her face fly-netted in the shadow of a mushroom-coloured hat I hadn't seen. Then the room was empty, the punkah fell loose from its moorings, her hat box left open on the floor.

She took to gardening in the night. I lay in bed listening to her snipping at maidenhair fern, the snap of her clippers pruning, the dull pulling of weeds. A branch she'd drag across the lawn in the dark. I got out of bed to take her lemon cordial and ginger biscuits on a tray. Sometimes she smiled as I came, other times she frowned vaguely like she wondered who I was. She'd drink and eat fast, still on her knees, looking around as though the food wasn't hers. Then return to her weeding, feeling the dirt and talking with plants as if I weren't there.

Once I thought it was her in the night but it was a longhorn steer loose in the garden, picking at the lawn and eating camellias. Then I found her too, in the shadows of the Moreton Bay fig, stealing water. She filled her hat from the tap at the tank. My father had told her she wasn't allowed. She walked furtively with a hatful to pour on the roses when there wasn't enough rain for bathing or drinking. She thought I was him but I wasn't. I didn't mean to frighten her.

Early in the newfallen mornings I heard her come in from her night gardening, sneaking past my father asleep in his chair. She thought he didn't see her, didn't know of her secret hat-watering. Then she started wandering off, out across the paddocks in her nightgown. She said she was going to see her parents, but they were still in Europe. He'd have to go out searching when the sun came up. Then he started keeping her inside, bolting her in the room with the lock I couldn't open. He knew I'd let her out if I had the key. He said she was using too much water but I knew it was worse than that. When she pounded at the door and talked all night, cursing him in languages he didn't understand, he strapped her in the bed, tied the palette in her mouth: a special snaffle bit with keys and a rubber plate that lay flat across the tongue. He first used it on a horse he bought for fifteen pounds at the Deniliquin market. He tied it around her neck with the tea towel I gave her for Christmas. It had a ship on it.

I sit in the ladder-backed chair and listen to the burr of the phone, think of the other end ringing in the house among the trees where it's three hours later. It's more than a year since I've seen her.

"Where are you?" Callie asks.

"Los Angeles."

"Why?"

I look out the window. The street is dark and slick. I didn't expect the rain. A car has its window taped with plastic.

"I took a bus from Baltimore," I say. "I wanted to be where you weren't."

The line is silent but for a crackling. I wonder how much she thinks about me. I wish I was drunk.

"What's it like there?" she asks.

"Depends what you're doing," I say.

Latin music comes from an apartment opposite. I can see people through a frosted skylight, like a party, but nobody dances.

"I tried stunt riding," I say. "They'd heard about me jumping cars. They had me jump on a horse from a building." I wait for her to say something back but she doesn't. "I told them horses aren't built for that."

The smell of dried pine wafts from the Christmas tree

that grows in a pot beside me. It still has its decorations from last year, a silver bird and plastic bells.

"They wanted me to jump a convertible Buick on a skewbald pony," I say.

"You need a decent horse for that," she says.

I pick up a pencil, it feels cold against my fingers. "I've been giving midweek ladies' riding lessons," I say. "Some of them have expensive horses." I make it sound better than it is. Every time I see a likely thoroughbred, I think of what Callie and I would make of it, how we'd school it over jumps, what we'd put in its mouth, a loose-ring snaffle or a soft rubber Pelham.

A woman walks along the street below me, her hair pinned up in a sort of nest. Her dress is flimsy for a rainy night. She has on what look like ballroom dancing shoes.

"The women here are different," I say. "Sort of brassy."

"Have you been with any?" she asks.

"Not yet."

The shadows from car lights extend along the buildings and then fade as they pass the end of the street.

"Where do you stay?" she asks.

"An apartment in Hollywood." I don't tell her it's "nightly and furnished," how there isn't a bed, just a vinyl chaise longue with a blanket and cushions. How they have big, uncomfortable buttons. I look at the unshaded lamp. The room makes me weary.

A dull noise breaks the quiet on the end of the phone. It sounds like a closing door.

"Are you alone?" I ask.

"Charlie Easterbrook's come home," she says.

"Is he the father or the son?"

"The father."

I wonder if she's still with Buddy Black, or if it's Charlie Easterbrook now. It's been more than a year that I've been with myself. I think about her all the time, as if she lives in a room inside my chest, a place I get my breath from.

"Do you miss me?" I say to the silence.

"You were the one who got on the bus," she says.

I bite down on the end of the pencil, taste the wood on my teeth. "You don't have to stay to be the one who's left behind," I say.

A group of men walks out of the apartment opposite. Black pants and white shirts, their hair slicked back from their faces, drunk enough to be happy.

"America's lonely without you," I say.

"You'll get used to it," she says.

The letter I wrote her is on the table beside me, the shape of my hand traced on the page when I didn't know what to say. A picture of a banjo player is on the wall, his shoes and shirt made from stuck-on bits of glitter, his face made up to look like he's smiling. How does she know what I'll get used to?

"I don't want to be here anymore," I say. I look out the window, the street is empty and quiet. "I'm going back where I came from."

"That's a bit drastic," she says, and then there is silence. She doesn't ask me to stay. "Are you in touch with your father?"

"Not 'specially," I say. There's a chill in the room, I feel it in my feet. I close the window with my free hand.

"You never told me what happened to your mother either," she says.

I press the side of my face to the cold closed window, against the street outside. I realise how little she knows about me, how little I've told her. "I watched her die," I say. I don't tell her how it happened. "It's been eleven years." I keep one ear tight to the receiver, the other against the glass as if listening for something else. The street is bare and still. My breathing sounds deliberate.

"If you'd planted a sapling there, it would be a tree by now," says Callie.

"My father would have cut it down."

I hear her breathing. "Don't go forever," she says.

PART TWO

Now there's a sign that says MAUDE before you get into town. A few dusty cars and dogs, the weatherboard store, the Maude Hotel with its bull-nosed veranda, and the square sandstone post office that used to seem so big.

The mail van driver turns from the bitumen road and pulls to a stop in the dirt outside the post office door. I take my suitcase from among the mail bags in the back. A truck rattles through on the road to Broken Hill.

I sit on the one dusty bench and close my eyes. It's hot and I'm tired. I'm not sure what I'll do if he doesn't come. I don't want to talk to the locals. I could hitchhike out there and see what's left, but nobody drives in that direction. The flies are loud as an echo in a pipe, and the heat is thick, the air just hangs in slabs. I wish Callie was here to dilute it somehow, as a decoy. She loves the heat, Hoofers used to call her Lizard.

A new sign above the general store says COVA COTTAGE in red. The blacksmith's shop is gone from over the road. There's a garage with a petrol pump in its place, and a feed store with a phone box outside. There is no one in the street.

I wind my watch nineteen hours ahead of Los Angeles time. It's ten to eleven on Thursday morning, 16 January 1958.

He gets out of a brown and white Vauxhall sedan in front of the general store, goes around to the boot of the car, opens it, and stands there. He looks shorter than I imagined. I pick up my case and walk towards him. He has on a fawn-coloured, long-sleeved shirt, buttoned at his wrists despite the heat, and a brown-checked hat with a peak. He wears dark glasses that don't suit him, but they hide his bunged-up eye.

I say "Hello" as I put my case in the trunk. Hands are not shaken. He is smaller, the way older people's necks recede into their shoulders. I left when I was twelve, he was taller than me then. I haven't seen him since.

I get in the passenger side and look over at him as he leans forward to start the car. "I guess you got my telegram," I say. He nods as the car crunches forward on the gravel. It smells vaguely of banana, as though there might be a peel blackening under the seat.

At the pub he takes a right onto the Burrabogie road out of town. As he turns the steering wheel, I watch the backs of his hands, freckled brown with sun and ingrained with dirt. It's hard to imagine them once young and pink and touching my mother.

It's hotter than I remember. Sweat pools on my shirt as it clings to the ribbed seat behind me. My legs itch in my trousers. I pull a knob that says "fan" in the hope that some air might circulate, but he reaches over and turns it off.

"Runs through petrol," he says. He's still not a generous man.

I wind down the window and rest my elbow, let in the

furnace from outside. “Bushfire weather,” I say, a bleak attempt at conversation.

The Murrumbidgee is low. The bridge is still unfenced but it’s now been cemented for cars. On the other side, Muddy Gates Lane is the same dusty track of a road, an unpuddled path through the mulga, named in a wet year; I’ve never seen it muddy. Once we’re on it, the body of the car shakes hard, dust comes up through the floor.

On the bench seat between us a stack of empty egg cartons, cupped one inside another, edges forward each time we hit a rut. He pulls out the armrest from its hole in the seat and lays it on top of them to keep them still. I take hold of the vinyl strap above the door.

“These windscreens shatter,” he says, slowing the Vauxhall down. The speed indicator changes from orange to yellow as the coloured line recedes across the dashboard. The windshield is shaped like a big, bent fish. The lane is nothing but bumps and ruts, there is no choice but to hit them. He slows enough so the tyres don’t skim the corrugations, they enter each of them deliberately.

My father starts parting and closing his lips; the spittle between them makes a sound like a drip from a tap. I want to put my fingers in my ears to avoid it and hum like I did as a child. Instead, I try and remember why I’m here. There are things I want. The photo of my mother by the fountain in the snow, the dress wound up in an Arnott’s biscuit tin. I left it under the boards where the milk separator stood on the meat safe floor. I want to visit her grave, plant something there.

The sign on the cypress tree at the gate still says PALPARARA. The house is the same but the garden is gone. My father takes a hand off the wheel and wipes his palm on his pants. The hand that didn't shake mine. I wonder if bits of truth will fall from him?

"Do you know I've been living in Los Angeles?" I ask. I don't mention Maryland. "It was a furnished apartment." I don't mention how, half asleep and sweating in the echo of the street, I saw images of my mother forming in the shapes and car-lit shadows in the ceiling above my bed, and in the breeze that shifted the light in the chintz of the curtains as they swelled along the wall. I look over at the squeezed-up man beside me as he stops the car in the shade outside the house and makes the tap-drip sound with his nervous live-alone lips.

"It must be noisy in America," he says.

The Dark Room is still as dark. It smells of mice and moth dust. I walk in and put my case down on the bed that was mine. There are three beds now, close together. Two of them are wooden. They weren't here before. Mine has an iron frame.

It's the only room in the house with curtains. Long, maroon velvet ones made by my mother. She sewed eyelets in them for rings and hung them on a rod. Now they are nailed along the top of the window, permanently drawn closed. It's not as hot in here as the rest of the house. The room is cooled by its darkness and the shade of the fig tree. The sound of the branches as they rub the corrugated roof above me is familiar.

My father has folded a moth-eaten blanket and a towel on the end of my bed. The towel is one I remember. It was softer then, the bridges of Europe printed on it weren't faded. I run my hand over it. The fabric is coarse from drying outside in the sun. There are peg marks pressed along its edge.

In the tall, mirrored wardrobe where I stood and touched my body as a boy, I see myself as I am now. I realise how America has made me handsome somehow, more self-conscious.

I imagine how I would look if I'd stayed here. Not as filled out perhaps, not standing as tall; my shoulders in front of my hips in the beginnings of a stoop, my face more beaten by weather. I wonder if in time I'll lose my neck and waist like my father, the spaces between my vertebrae closing up.

In the mirror I see the redness in my eyes. It took me two days to get here. Twenty-seven hours on a Qantas flight to Honolulu, to Papeete, then Auckland, and Melbourne.

An old Chinaman was beside me on the bus from Spencer Street Station up the Hume to the Riverina. He looked strange among the flabby-faced women and the men in broad-brimmed hats. I sat with him to avoid their stories. Beside him I felt less foreign. I watched the gum trees rush by on either side. He was the only other one on board who flinched each time the bus hit a kangaroo on the highway. He spoke no English, just offered me a purple sweet wrapped in grease paper. I pretended to eat it but stuck it between the seats. I tried not to think about Callie.

At the depot in Deniliquin, before he got off the bus, he nodded to me and gave me a red bookmark with Chinese characters, a golden Buddha printed on it.

I need to shower. I don't want to wake up dirty in my clothes. I take the towel from the bed and walk out into the passage. The room across the hall where my mother died is still bolted. There's now a shiny silver padlock on it. I wonder if it was added for my arrival.

There's a church pew curved along the wall. An unlikely addition. My mother's clock from Europe hangs above it. It still ticks loudly but the hands have both fallen to six-thirty and don't seem to move.

The door to the bathroom doesn't have a bolt. I push

a marble-topped table of my mother's against it. My father has brought in a bath. I look at it, all hooked up and functional. A shallow puddle has formed in the hairs and other skerricks of his last wash. As the hot tap gushes rusty water, I kneel over the side and swill out the scunge. Once the water begins to clear and run hot I push in the plug and get in, allowing the bath to draw up around me.

There is a flue in the ceiling where the steam is supposed to go. The light that comes in through it reflects around my feet. My nails need trimming. I had to go to America to learn to clip them.

I hear my father in the hallway, pushing at the bathroom door. The jammed-up table scrapes an inch or so across the floor. His grubby fingers curve around the edges, scabs on his knuckles.

"I'm in the bath," I say, sitting up abruptly, water spilling above the lip. He can't hear me. "I'm in here." I say it louder and he stops.

The fly-wire side door shuts. I can see him through the cobwebbed window. His shoulders humped, he pisses from the veranda. I watch him through the window, peeing weakly in the dirt outside. A buckled-up old man who put a towel and blanket on my bed.

"What's it like there?" my father asks, pouring treacle in his tea. I sit catty-corner from him in the kitchen with a glass of tank water. The table is covered with linoleum that matches the floor. It has a pattern of bricks, worn thin to the wood where his elbows are.

"The heat is dry like here, but not as hot. Some people have air-conditioning," I tell him. I talk about Los Angeles as if I'd been there all the time.

"What's that for?" he asks. I can't believe he doesn't know.

"It's like a fan in the wall with water."

He dips a gingernut biscuit in his tea, studies it, and puts it in his mouth.

"I train horses at a stable beside the Los Angeles River," I say. "It's been cemented up so it's more like a drain."

He spits on the tips of his fingers and rubs them in the tarnish on the teapot.

"They have gum trees in Los Angeles," I say. I think of the women I was teaching, sweaty-headed, talentless, determined under the brims of hunting caps, their ponytails going limp. I don't tell my father I still have no driver's licence or bank, that I carry my money and passport on me, strapped around my middle in a nylon belt with a pocket that tucks in the front of my underpants. I still don't mention Maryland.

"Gum trees!" he says, then grunts.

"They call them eucalyptus," I tell him.

A school of flies has settled on the treacle spoon. My father waves them off and puts the spoon back in the tin.

"They hardly have flies in L.A.," I say.

The woodstove sits in the wall, rusted brown as the hull of a raised-up boat. On the griddle is a two-handled pot, the one my mother used for parsnip soup. I slide my chair and poke my head in over the top. Cold porridge has gone dark in the bottom.

"What do you do there?" he asks. I've already told him. I skid back to the table and watch the wrigglers swimming in my water glass, wondering if they'll blossom into mosquitoes in my belly or intestines. I miss tank water.

"I go to the beach," I say.

He turns and squints at me as though it's unlikely.

I went once. To Santa Monica. It was too late to learn to like it. My legs were so pale that I stayed in my corduroy pants. I sat for a while on a canvas chair and read a copy of *Practical Horseman*. Then I went down and stood where the waves wet the sand. Water rolled in and swallowed up my feet and the ground shifted out from under my sandals as it ran back out. Flotsam of corks and bits of washed-up cloth. Beach children ran past me and dived through the froth, into the dark where the seaweed circled. The movement made me queasy. I had to look away, up to where the sand was dry, towards the colours of the cliffs and sunbathers on the beach. The water was freezing. The bottoms of my trousers were wrinkled and salty. I folded the chair and left.

~

I imagine the beach at Rehoboth, dotted with all her washed-up horses, good horses, Flanagan, Whistler, Canadian Bay, bloated on the sand, like sweaters full of wind on a clothesline. I run down to help them. A spike in the abdomen—I've seen it done with sheep. It leaves them flat as sacks.

Callie laughs at me from somewhere as I run from the swill of the waves. She's got the engine running in the car up on the foreshore. She says they're dead and she's ready to go home. She's eating unwashed carrots from a bag.

I think of things I never told her, how she's as variable as weather, how she has talent without grace, how I've dreamt of making love to her on the lawn at Lower Wye, the plastic scarf around her neck. How I can't help thinking about who she sleeps with now.

I could tell her about the horses here, how they wander wild and wormy, like hat racks in the desert. I could tell her what's left of the garden, how the cypress trees are all but gone, a leggy camellia, the familiar smell of the septic tank, the black-eyed Susan that grows from a seep and spreads across the concrete lid like a veil. I sit up against the dark and wonder if she'd like it here, my childhood strewn about me like so many rocks.

If she's still at Charlie Easterbrook's, it would be ten

o'clock at night her time, it would still be yesterday. I walk down the passage, past the linen closet, everything dusty and untouched. The hall light sheds on places I would hide in as a child, where I lay along shelves and underneath things. I'd appear from the dark like a secret. The Creeping Jesus.

I kneel by the phone stool and fumble along the skirting for the socket and connection. My father leaves the phone unplugged, he doesn't like it ringing. From the stool I dial enough zeros for directory long distance, recite the string of numbers. "I'll pay for it here," I say to the operator.

"What are you doing?" my father asks from behind me. I didn't expect he would hear.

"Using the phone," I say.

"Local?"

I shake my head and listen to the ringing, the receiver feels cold on my ear.

"Who you calling?"

I pretend not to hear him, concentrate hard on the phone. I turn my body but he doesn't leave or come closer.

"Who's paying?" he asks.

Someone picks up and says hello, a man's voice I don't recognise.

"Is Callie there?"

No, he says, but I can hear her in the background, laughing with someone else. It sounds like a party, it sounds like a long way away. She'll be back in June, says the man, and then starts laughing himself. I can't tell if he's drunk or if he's joking, or if he knows it's me.

"What sort of name is that?" my father asks.

I listen for her voice in case she's coming but there's no answer, just the sound of people talking. Then the line goes dead. I don't hang up or turn around, I pretend that I'm still waiting. My father stands at the door.

"Where is she?" he asks.

I put down the phone and look at him. I shake my head without saying.

I sit on the wooden veranda. It seems strange to write to Callie on my mother's stationery.

Palparara, via Maude, New South Wales. I form the words deliberately, European loops and curves my mother taught me, not like American printing. Callie who writes like a child.

My father scuffs down towards the yards, his leather slippers on. It's the time of day when he fills the trough and feeds his favourite horse. He throws it a biscuit of hay, brushes himself of the seeds that fly back on his shirt-sleeves. He turns on the tap in the trough and waits with one hand in the water.

I look at the writing paper, the curled-up corners, and then stare into the sharpness of the sun. I wonder if she's with the man who answered the phone, if he knew who I was from my accent. I don't write the things I've wanted to.

My father shuffles back up the drive, rubs his hand on the woven-wire gate as he passes, looks at the rust on his thumb. He nods to acknowledge he's seen me. "Writing to that girl with the name?" he asks. I angle the page so he can't see. "Did you tell her why you're here?"

"Why am I here?" I ask him.

He looks at the box of my mother's moth-eaten paper that sits on the steps beside me. "Sniffing around the past,

I suppose," he says, a dullness in his tone. He leans down and picks up an unused postcard from the box. A stuffed Tasmanian tiger, dry about the eyes, stuck among the trees for the postcard photo as though it's still alive.

"Looks more like a dog than a cat," I say.

He narrows his eyes at it. "They're supposed to be extinct," he says.

"Do you have envelopes?" I ask him.

He looks down at my half-written letter. "I don't correspond," he says. I fold it as though it's finished. "Did you invite the girl out here?" he asks.

"She has her own fish to fry."

"They usually do," he says. He puts the postcard in his pocket. "You should get some fish of your own."

“Do you know Mother had a miscarriage in the billabong?” I ask my father. We’re at the kitchen table. I don’t look over at him.

“She lost a lot of babies,” he says. He gets up to rinse his cup and leaves the room.

I don’t answer; I didn’t know there were other lost babies. I put my glass in the sink with the dishes and open kitchen cupboards until I find a rusted can of Mortein flyspray, in with the jam and Vegemite, and take it with me to bed.

I never minded mosquitoes in the night until I lived without them. They drone around the bedroom in the dark like single-engine planes. I spray the room and then up the chimney until it’s toxic and quiet.

In the bed, I breathe through the filter of the blanket, taste the insecticide settled in the back of my throat, and sleep. The room separates from the house and goes to sea but it’s not waterproof; waves break against the window, octopuses and seaweed floating. It runs aground on a beach where people in old-fashioned bathers peer through the window. Their startled expressions wake me. But there is nothing, the curtains are still drawn. The shadows of the wind in the tree through the thinning material, the scratch of a twig on the glass, then the sound of my father walking.

Footfalls, out the side door and into the garden. My watch says a quarter to two.

I slip on my boxers and sandals and follow, out to the veranda and under the drape of the Moreton Bay fig. I watched my mother from here.

He stands at the chopping stump beside the woodshed, turns the grinding wheel and sharpens the splitting axe. Sparks fly as he touches the blade on the stone. For a moment his face is lit in the dark, his good eye bright like a lamp from a distant window.

The blade sharp, he begins to split wood as though he's pressed for time; twelve-inch lengths for the boiler. Each slice of the axe into the dead pine echoes, chips, and splinters. He cocks his head, turning it to focus on each upright log as he swings. When the splitter sticks in the timber he jerks it free, using his foot against the wood if he has to. He is a good axeman still.

With twenty or so logs already done, he plants the axe a final time, the blade deep in the stump, and loads what he's cut on the wheelbarrow. He pushes the barrow fully laden through the remains of the garden. The iron wheel is without tread or rubber and it doesn't run well through the rough, but he pushes anyway, heaving it over the beds where flowers once grew. He makes new paths, over where her begonias were, where there was a line of camellias, through the pampas grass in the overgrown beds that once were filled with irises and roses.

The sky is flat and low above him, the night too hot for pushing a barrow without a reason. The cattle dogs are restless on their chains. They know that timber gets chopped in daylight, that the way from the woodshed to the boiler woodbox isn't fifteen reckless shapes around the garden until he can't go further.

Maude is still a town without a church. There is no statue in a park or bridge across a river. My father parks the car under a stand of gum trees. I post the letter to Callie, even though it says things that are slightly sarcastic, like how are your horses swimming? Four stamps with owls on them, eight eyes looking.

I follow my father across the parking lot to the hotel; he protects his eye from the dust of a passing utility truck. "You could get an eyepatch," I tell him.

"It's too far from the sea to look like a pirate," he says.

The pub is dark inside. An old aboriginal woman sits at the end of the bar in a sailor's hat with a cigarette drooped from her lip. Smoke curls from the end of it, then spreads in the breeze from the ceiling fan that stirs the air above her.

"Ginger Rogers," my father says as we walk in, motioning in the old woman's direction. He doesn't take off his hat.

Other locals are in the lounge, sitting around tables eating porterhouse steaks and coleslaw. My father doesn't notice them and they don't talk to him.

A bearded man looks around at us and then averts his eyes. He leans forward, telling something to the people he's with. I imagine the rumours of my father: the wife dead without a funeral, something strange about him since the bull kick queered his eye.

I sit near Ginger Rogers on a stool beside my father. He orders a beer from a tall woman in moleskin trousers standing behind the bar. She turns around and is Leonie, eleven years later. Her hair has gone from red to a rusty grey. She puts a strand of it behind her ear, smiles at him, and then sees me.

"Hello, Day," she says with widened eyes.

My father combed his hair across his head, he shaved and changed his shirt before we came, but he never said Leonie would be here.

I don't know what to say to her. I search for a glimpse of my mother in her eyes, the way I sometimes do with older women; in the twist of a blond sheath of hair or a braid like she would wear before bed, in an accent from Austria or Hungary, or the blue of her dress in the colour of a cushion. But there's none of this in Leonie, just the passing of years, an awkwardness caused by my stare.

"Get him a beer," my father tells her.

"I'll have a cranberry juice."

"Did you bring the cranberries with you?" he asks me, sharing his smirk with Leonie.

"A lemonade's fine," I say.

She pours it fizzy from a bottle into a tall glass, plops a glazed cherry in it, and sits it on a coaster in front of me.

"In America you get ice without asking," I say. Leonie smiles but doesn't offer me any.

I watch my father sip his beer. He follows Leonie's arm

as it wipes across the bar. She still has farmer's fingers. The nails are bitten, the skin around them rough. She's wearing my mother's oblong watch.

"You don't drink?" she asks me, her voice throaty.

"A horse somersaulted on me," I tell her. "It split my liver."

"Doesn't your liver grow back?" my father asks. I thought he wasn't listening.

Leonie pulls the tap and angles another glass for the right amount of head. She mixes two Bundaberg rum and Cokes, puts them on a tray.

"Are you still riding?" I ask her.

"Sometimes I go up to the squatter's hut with your father," she says and takes the tray out to a table. I remember them there, shunting on the bed above me.

"What do you think of how she's fixed the hotel lounge?" my father says.

"Nice carpet," I tell him.

The carpet has a pattern for all occasions. There are frosted lights stuck around the walls. I look up and watch the wobble of the ceiling fan, listen to it creaking, imagine the day it struggles free from its moorings, careens across the room decapitating lunchers.

"I hid under the bed up in the hut when you were with her," I turn and tell my father. He looks at me as though he doesn't know whose room or bed I'm talking about.

I get up to go outside for air, pass Leonie on the way. She would be pretty with makeup, if her hair was cut and off her face. She would attract more than my father. She still wears pants the same. I see her freckled hands around the tray. She's taken off the watch.

Out in the car park, the air is getting thicker. Floats of nimbus build, an outside chance of rain. I can feel my father standing in the doorway behind me.

"Looks like rain," I tell him.

"Looks like clouds," he says.

Sometimes they come in dark with the tease of distant thunder, then roll right past to rain on someone else; on shady farms with green-grassed hills on the edges of the Great Dividing Range. Or if it starts to rain, the unseasoned will run outside and raise their hands up to it—until they realise it's hitting too hard, water running across the ground in search of rivers, taking the last of the topsoil with it, scalding the backs of horses.

I walk with my father to the car.

"I think I'll stay in town, make my own way back," I tell him. He doesn't look at me, he doesn't want me alone with Leonie.

I slap the roof of the Vauxhall as he drives off in the dust. The town is flat and empty, I watch the car get smaller.

A single drop of rain puts a dent in the dirt beside me. Looking up I see a stream of sun between two grey-bellied clouds, sheds of corrugated light refracting above them, gilding their edges. "A glimpsing of heaven" my mother once called it, her unusual English, pointing up from her garden, her other hand shading her face.

I go back inside. Downstairs is for drinking, people stay upstairs. I follow the many-coloured carpet up along the banister, three stairs at a time, around a landing to the second floor, looking for Leonie's room. Unseen, I open the door that has PRIVATE painted on it. It is hers. On the dresser is a recent picture of her riding with my father.

More comforts than I'd imagined. The bed has four posts without a canopy, a tablecloth drapes the window, softening the sun.

My mother's Queen Anne chair is beside the bed, the one she'd sit in and sew. Its velvet has been replaced by dark green vinyl. I sit down in it and look around. Fake leather clams against my legs.

I slide open the bedside table drawer. In it there's a silver matchbox cover, some unused Irish postcards, and, in the back, a small dark book. My mother's initials and the year 1916 in blotted ink on the brown canvas jacket. It feels rough and smells old, the gold-edged pages frayed, silverfish. It reads from back to front. The inside cover says "Daily Prayers According to the Custom, Published Jos. Guns, Vienna, 1857." The rest is in a language I haven't seen; the alphabet is strange, notes in the margin, back-to-front letters, many of them dotted.

When I was very small, I woke up in the night to the sound of my mother murmuring. My father wasn't home. Through the crack of her bedroom door I watched her sitting on bare boards, her hair in a braid, her face unpowdered, lit in the flicker of candles. A shawl-like garment wrapped around her, she looked like someone else, reading in a low-pitched voice, words I didn't understand.

I hear someone in the hall, slide the book down the

front of my pants. Leonie comes in and finds me standing by her bed.

"What are you up to?" she asks.

"I'm looking for my mother's watch."

She hands it to me casually from the pocket of her shirt as though it's just a trinket. "She died a long time ago," she says, gives me a hug I don't anticipate, her arms around me hard. It's as if to say she understands. She feels the book against her in my trousers.

"What's in your pants?" she asks.

"Her book."

I look outside. The clouds are plumper, eclipsing the sun. Softly, it is starting to rain, spotting the dusty window. Leonie pulls at an eyebrow, not sure what to say.

"Your mother was a Jewess," she says.

I leave Leonie in her room and walk slowly down the stairs, the watch tight in my hand, warm and silver in my fingers, the book still in my pants. I hadn't met Jews until I went to America. My father doesn't like them.

He's in the kitchen cooking toasted cheese and Vegemite like it's Chicken à la King. I sit at the table, finishing a game of patience. The cards have pictures of English hunting scenes.

"What do you think about Jews?" I ask him. He doesn't look away from his frypan.

"I didn't know she was one when I married her," he says, as though he's not to blame. "She wanted to go back to Vienna, but it wasn't safe, the War wasn't over."

"She was safe here?"

"This is where she belonged," he says.

"You belong here," I say. I get up and go to my room, sit on the bedspread from my childhood, my twelve-year-old's stains. I run my fingers across the familiar bobbles and knotted cotton, the patches where it's worn quite flat. It looks like a faded relief map. Some children here are born in the Bush Nursing Hospital, others at home on kitchen tables. I was born on a boat. I was circumcised. I wonder if there was a doctor on board. Were there candles in her cabin, a small operation, a baby crying? Did she whisper Hebrew prayers while she helped him keep my body still, whiskey or gin on the cotton wool, his scissors sharp for cutting?

My mother was as fair as me. Turning my head in the

wardrobe mirror, I look for the Jew in my face. My nose is prominent but there's nothing of it in my colouring. I wonder how Jews are supposed to look.

She placed a star of sticks on top of where she put the baby, buried before it formed a bone or feature. I remember how she walked, awkward like she wished she had more clothes to cover her. The next day there was an oval stone and twigs, arranged in the dirt in the shape of a star. She'd been down at the edge of the water in the dark.

A sheath of light dapples down the ladder to the bottom of the tank. Lank strands of algae lean and weave in less than an ankle of water. A big fish wends its way towards the shape the light makes, stops and sucks at air. Mottled brown and black, with a pink, appaloosa mouth. It must be ten inches long.

"There's a big old fish in the drinking water," I tell my father. He's standing in the part of the porch that is fly-wired, watching me through the mesh.

"You put it there," he says.

The year the billabong went dry. A muddy little fish, an inch long, flopping in a stagnant puddle, a cattle dog crouched on its haunches, yelping. I shooed the dog and cupped my hands with the mucky water, scooped out the fish and walked it up the paddock to the tank.

We'd had a load of water delivered on the back of a Bedford truck, it cost my father fifteen quid. "Drought prices," the truck driver called it. My mother was already stealing it for the garden, a bucket on the end of a rope in the night. Every morning for a month I dropped in bread-crumbs. I didn't know my father saw me. The fish would swim to the light and eat them. I called it Shadrach after a horse that died.

"Fish don't live for fifteen years," I tell my father.

"Fish live forever," he says. "Grow to the size of what surrounds 'em."

The fish is as big as the bucket I carry it in. Its gaze is unblinking, up at the sky, like the stare from my father's glassy eye. The billabong doesn't go dry like it used to. I remember a water diviner named Vickers came through with a forked stick and coat-hanger wire, told my father to drill the bottom, open up the spring. It filled back up, grew to twice its size.

I set the old carp free, back where it came from. It lies on its side for a bit in the shallow, swims gingerly into the reeds. I see my reflection, rippled slightly by the movement. I haven't put my head under water except in a bath since the day my mother lost the baby. More than fifteen years. It might be safe to go in now. There is no rip or undertow, the water is heavy and still. I drop my shirt and corduroys in the dirt beside me. My foot in the water, it's warm and enticing. I look to see if my father has followed. I don't want anyone seeing that I can't swim.

"Do your legs like frogs do," my mother said. "Do the stroking slowly." She swam breaststroke.

Once my head is under I want to do it fast, it's only thirty feet. I tear clumsily with open fingers, both breaststroke and freestyle at once. I feel the panic in my chest, it doesn't let me breathe. Reeds wrap my neck and elbows, a lily pad slaps my face. I stop and look up to see where I am. I've gone deeper than I wanted. I reach with a foot to see if I can stand but there's nothing as the water parts, folds me in, thick as malt molasses in my throat. Exhaustion comes quickly. As I flail against it, it's not how I thought it would happen. I look up at a last wet corner of sky; I'm like a stone that seeks the bottom. It is dark and I am drowning.

Sudden hands burst my head above the level, a drag under my armpits, the scrape of heels in clay, my head laid on a rock. I look up at the yellow-white nothing above me, then I see him squatting nearby. He wipes his mouth along his arm, walks on up the paddock, his hat back on his head, sopping wet and heavy in his clothes. He leaves me naked in the mud to make my own arrangements.

"A wet arse and no fish," my father says, back up at the house. He's sitting in his living room chair, drinking instant coffee, hugging the cup like it's keeping him warm. He's changed into his boiler suit, a twisted hanky on his head. His sodden pants and work shirt are wrung out and hanging on the fireguard, his hat is hung and dripping from the rack.

I sit on the couch, my back still caked with clay, my skin wet through. The fire sheds a heat that turns my dampness into sweat and still I shiver.

"I didn't know you couldn't swim," he says. He must have come down running; he's old to come so quickly. I opened my eyes and he was kneeling over me, fully clad and dripping. He didn't speak, I didn't move.

"Don't drink, don't swim," he says. He smiles as he works the bellows. I've never seen him pleased with himself. He squeezes out the elastic sides of his boot, watches each drip sizzle as it hits the hearth, then stares back at the flames. "No more fish piss in the drinking water," he says. "Gives you English teeth."

He tends the fire, I watch his hands around a log. "In America it's all chlorine and fluoride. All those white-teeth people, smiling all over you," he says.

I lick my crusted lips. There's a taste of his tobacco dried around my mouth. I hadn't realised how he saved me. The strange humiliation of his pipe-stale breath inside me. I don't remember his touch when I was young, he didn't shake my hand when I arrived, didn't hold me as a baby.

"Where did you learn the mouth-to-mouth?" I ask him.

"On a river as a kid. In Scotland. My brother," he says. "It didn't work on him." I didn't know he had a brother. Looking at his trousers hanging as they dry, I picture a ruddy-faced boy in the rain, running in hand-me-down shorts along the tracks that lead him home.

The new log makes the fire crack and spit. A small hole burns in the raggedy hearth rug; neither of us moves to stamp it. We watch it smoulder into nothing.

"Was he older or younger, your brother?" I ask.

"Two years older."

"What was his name?"

"Derry," he says, staring at flames. "Derry down Derry. It all went different after that."

My father wants help in the paddock over the road. "Grubbing thistles," he calls it. "Before it gets too hot." He climbs the stile out past the compost heap, carries a sharp-edged hoe on his shoulder.

We walk out into the flats towards a spot he points to, where thistles are seeding and blighting one side of the paddock. My father is bandy-legged from long days spent on horses, his elastic-side boots worn down on the outsides. His feet are strong as hooves.

"What was with Mother and Dickie Del Mar?" I ask him as we walk. I wish I'd started with small talk.

"She knew him in Europe. I thought he was a poofter at first," he says.

"Why?"

"His moustache, the hat."

"He was from Argentina," I say.

"The way he fixed food, had flowers in his room," he says. "His hair was cut straight across the back."

We come to a patch of Scotch thistles, prickly stems and purple flowers, seeds that float in tufts like those of dandelions. He starts grubbing at the roots with his hoe. I have a mattock, shaped like a pickaxe, but the end is broad instead of pointed. The clay soil doesn't dig easily.

I wipe my brow with my shirtarm, wondering why I

wore sleeves. "I never told Mother he drowned," I say.

My father turns up to look at me. The sun reflects for a breath in his good eye until he looks back down. "That wasn't him. It was some bloke riding through, he had a brown horse and a hat like Dickie's. Got caught in the water."

"You made me think it was him," I say.

"I never said it was."

"I was nine years old," I say.

"You were more his than mine." He looks away sharply and strikes his hoe in the dirt. My breath gets shoved up in my chest. "He never really loved her," he says.

"Are you saying he's my father?" My voice feels loud but it isn't.

He stops but doesn't look up, pulls at his ear. "Sleeping dogs get up eventually," he says.

"Why didn't anyone tell me?" I look down at the fresh-hit thistle stems.

"He was a gutless wonder."

"I still have dreams of him up in that tree," I say.

He nods into the dirt. "He knew Emily was mine." I've never heard him call her by her name.

"Why didn't he take me with him?"

"He only wanted her." Thistledown floats around us like planets.

"Where is he now?"

"He doesn't keep me posted," he says. He takes his hoe and walks for home, as if he's the one who should be upset. The brindle dog gets up and follows. I'm left standing on my own, pieces of ground ripped out around me. “We’re not finished,” I say, but he doesn’t hear me, only the dog turns around.

Dickie Del Mar sat at the edge of the shed where the broken hay bales had fallen. He'd only been there a week. He arrived when I was nine. It was 1944. I wasn't sure where he came from or what he was doing at our place. My mother said she knew him in Vienna.

I stood by the tank stand and watched him. He was plaiting leather to make an Argentine bridle, weaving six strands together to make a headpiece and cheek straps in one.

"You can make the reins," he said. I couldn't tell if he took an interest in me so my mother would like him better, or if he liked me himself.

I sat opposite him and began braiding three thick strips into one. The kelpie dog came and sat beside me, rested its head on my foot. I tried imitating the way Dickie's fingers glided around the leather.

"Where did you come from?" I asked him. I leant into the shade from the shed.

His arms were smooth, shiny in the heat; he didn't have hair on them, they weren't thick like my father's.

"Different places. The Maldives."

I nodded slowly like I'd heard of it. It sounded like a hot place.

"I don't like the sun," I said.

"You're like your mother," he said. He smiled to himself, pulled at a thread of leather with his teeth. "She's a creature of the shade."

"Where did you meet her?" I asked.

"In Vienna. Near the station."

His fingers were long, like lizards, pale on the undersides. The way they moved made me want to reach over and touch them.

"She was buying flowers," he said. He seemed pleased to talk about it. "I bought her a cream gardenia."

I had the feeling that all gardenias were cream, my mother had them in her garden, but I didn't say anything.

"They were already married," he said. "It was after Darwin had left."

The edges of the leather were staining the sweat between my fingers. It looked like blood from a cut drying brown.

"How did you know to come here?" I asked.

"Your mother wrote me a letter before I left Europe."

He looked down the drive and into the paddocks.

"That was once all ocean," I said, motioning with my head. "There are specks of shells in the sand."

"The Great Inland Sea," he said. He already knew. He twisted two strands for a throat latch.

I could see my father riding in, his shape in the haze above the saltbush. I moved a bit further into the shade.

"Why were you in the Maldives?" I tried to pronounce it like I'd said it before. I wanted to find out more before my father got back. Dickie didn't talk to me when he was around.

"I was avoiding the War," he said. "Then I came out here, got a job on a Hereford stud in the Widden Valley. All the local cattlemen were joining up."

"Is it safe here?" I asked him.

"The Japs won't get this far. The Americans are in the Pacific."

"My father said he can't fight in the War," I said. "Not with a gammy eye."

I watched my father in the distance struggling with the gate into the paddock he calls Smiggins, his horse not standing still. Dickie still hadn't noticed him, he was too busy making his bridle. He looped one length he'd braided through itself and around each ring of the bit.

"No buckles, no stitches," he said.

"My father doesn't like you," I said.

He smiled again but he didn't answer. My father said Dickie was lazy, called him an afternoon farmer.

Dickie cut another thin strip with his palette knife from the sheet of soft Indian leather, carving it finely like stringing a bean, the blade towards his thumb. My father was now at the gate into the yards.

"It's dangerous cutting like that," I said.

"You can do dangerous things if you're good at them," he said.

My birthday wasn't celebrated in front of my father. My mother said he didn't like them. She'd make me a cupcake in the middle of June, so long as he wasn't around. There was no talk of a party, no kids from town to tag tails on donkeys, no blowing out candles, eyes scrunched shut for wishes. If I asked her exactly, she said the day didn't matter. There wasn't a calendar to circle it on.

Dickie decided to have a birthday party of his own. His was 12 November. He put on a dark velvet jacket and a red silk shirt, he grilled great skirts of steak on a griddle outside, bathed them in a sauce from his saddlebag pocket that tasted like spicy hot chutney.

Mother baked a black and tan cake that crumbled; we stuck it together with apricot jam, poked a lead pencil in its middle, and lit it in the kitchen as a candle. She came outside in her long evening dress, held the cake up like a trophy in the afternoon sun. Dickie snuffed the candle with his whole mouth around it, made a quick wish as if it was nothing.

"The wishing comes first, before the candle blowing," my mother said. "You're upside down." But Dickie didn't care.

Secretly with myself, I made a wish too: that he would take us away.

Dickie sipped a hot-brewed drink called yerba mate from a sherry tumbler, mixed it with whiskey poured from a flask he kept on the end of a fob in his jacket. Mother picked him a pink-rimmed azalea, placed it up in his lapel. We ate and he drank. They spoke French about things in Europe. It was like they had a secret language.

After we ate, Dickie set up the gramophone in the wide-open window, secured with a brick in the sill. He slid his Carlos Gardel record from its brown paper cover, as though it was an ancient plate of blackened pearl. He wound the crank so the turntable spun. The music crackled around in the late afternoon. I asked if it could be my birthday too.

Dickie scooped me up for a tango. He skirted me around, along the veranda, over the edge and down the cooch grass slope. He held me high, my feet flew free. The side of my face pressed close in the sweat and hairs on his chest, among the open buttons and the silk of his shirt. The sour-smelling drink was on his breath, the record was jumping at the scratches. He built them right into the rhythm of his struts and dives. His wide riding hand solid across my back, he dipped me so low my hair touched the stones on the path.

My mother watched from the brick arms of the steps, her dress puffed up around her. He swooped me close past her, my head in her lap as he knelt in a pose. She kissed my brow and he nuzzled her cheek, then danced me off down the path and into the long agapanthus.

"Stay away from my plants," my mother called, laughing.

"Agapanthus tango," he said, taunting her. He let me down deep in their leaves. He knew she didn't mind; it was him. I got up from them giddy, like I'd been swinging a broom, saw my father ride up the cart path, in through the Bracken Paddock gate. Mother saw him too, turned off the music, and began cleaning up the food. Dickie stamped at the remains of the fire.

We pretended to be sensible, as though the scratchy sounds of tango couldn't be heard for thirty acres, like smoke didn't rise from the fire.

My father walked past us and into the house. "It's a 'Total Fire Ban Day,' " he turned and said to me, as though the other two weren't there. There was the faintest snort from Dickie's throat as he swallowed up laughter. I had to bite my cheeks to stop my own. My mother looked down into her lap.

I pull at the ivy that wraps around the bricks and sucks its roots in tiny cups onto the boards of the meat safe door. The fly-wire has rusted in its mullions, a brown key sags from the lock.

I open the door as though someone might be inside. Dirt patches in the bottom of the bath have formed and stayed. When I remember her face, it's the clayed-up one from when I dreamt she lay here, tiny flowers from a wedding bush crowned around her head.

Under the milk separator is where I hid the biscuit tin, in a space between floor slabs—the red and white pattern on it, the name "Arnott's" across the lid, the picture of shortbread fingers. It's still there. Inside, her dress is balled up, roses left hanging on threads. The small, shining stone she gave me falls from its folds. The ruddy-coloured garnet feels familiar in my hand.

In the bottom of the tin lies the sepia photo of her standing alone by the fountain in the snow, her simple wedding dress, not enough to cover her in the cold. As I wipe dust from it I notice the brown paper backing has peeled away from the frame. Behind the photo there is writing. I tear it further. "*To Emily, Love forever, Alphonse Del Mar.*"

The car horn sounds outside, my father is waiting to

go. Pushing the dress back into the tin, I slip the picture from the frame and curl it up my shirtsleeve. I smuggle myself through the door and lock it, pass the fallen trellis where my mother tried growing passion fruit vines. I put the key in my pocket along with the stone.

My father wants to check if aborigines are back, squatting in the boundary hut where Leonie lived. I look over at him as he drives; I know his profile better than I know his face.

"Where did you meet Mother?" I ask him. He shifts around his seat, still not accustomed to questions. I know the answer, she told me.

"The opera in Montreux," he says. "Summer of '34." I don't ask more, I wait for him to offer it. "She was singing," he says.

We rumble over the cattle grid into the lane. Box thorn has taken over along the fence line, grass parrots leave the ground.

"Was Dickie Del Mar at the wedding?"

He looks over at me oddly, a turn of his head so he can focus with his good eye. "She met him after I left. I came out here to find a place."

We turn right along the river flat, bump between the anthills that pock the plain, head up in the direction of the hut. I wait for more.

"Her parents came to the wedding," he says. "I promised them I'd have her back within two years."

He concentrates hard on the windshield, slows as a Hereford bullock saunters across in front of us. I feel the picture against my forearm. It doesn't make sense. She wouldn't have married again, or were they playing dress-up, my mother and Dickie Del Mar?

I turn my arm and with my fingers quietly separate the cuff-slit that runs from the button up my sleeve, sneak a look at her faded face in the picture. She doesn't seem like she was playing. There's a pale bewilderment about her, as though she is alone.

Through the red gums and wedding bush the hut comes into view. My father parks in the shade of a boxgum, clunks the car door shut with a foot out behind him. I lean on the bonnet and watch him walk inside. I listen to a hint of breeze high up in the stringy barks, a quiet shushing through the leaves. The place looks empty and depressing. There is no sign of aborigines, other than a cotton singlet in the dust, an empty rice-pudding can, and the remains of a fire beneath the window. A half-burnt chair, quite a good wicker one, sits in the coals. He kneels down to see if the ashes are still warm. Disgusted, he walks back to the car.

"Bastards burn the furniture," he says.

He sits low in the driver's seat without starting the engine. I watch his wrinkled fists as they clamp around the wheel.

"Right after the wedding, I came on ahead to look for land," he nods into the distance. "She followed later. Arrived with you." He stops talking for a moment, choosing his words. "She said you were born before she left. I didn't believe her. It took her three months getting here."

She told me I was born on the boat she came out on.

He didn't know I was coming.

"She got here in August, a year since I'd seen her. She pretended you were three months old." Nine months pregnant, plus three; I do the maths in my head. "But you were so tiny I knew you were less," he says. "Only horses stay pregnant eleven months."

The features on his face are drawn and sad. I feel as though I should be happy that I'm not his, but tears are in the edges of my eyes.

Half a cup of rolled oats, three quarters of water and one of milk, a pinch of salt in my palm. I cook porridge like I did as a boy, after Dickie had gone and Leonie had come. I'd light the potbelly stove and make slow porridge for my mother. Sometimes she didn't get up, especially on Saturdays. I'd stir the mixture around a burnt-out saucepan, wait for it to get gluggy. I took tastes from the wooden spoon, blew on it to make it cool. I liked the furry taste of the wood.

My mother drifted in, wrapped in her long white robe, her hair still down and undone. She stared at the walls like I wasn't there. I poured her porridge from the pot; it looked like pale boiling mud.

"Where was I born?" I asked her.

She looked as though she was surprised that someone was attached to the pot; she searched my face before she answered.

"Somewhere off Mauritius, out in the Indian Ocean," she said with a halfhearted throw of her chin towards the window, as though it might be in that direction.

I pretended it was my birthday, 12 November, even though I knew it was in June. It was the day Dickie had his. I took gingernut snaps and lemon cordial in a Mason jar, passion fruit ripe from the vine. I climbed the cypress tree, made a table on four short boards laid across the branches, put a gingham napkin down as cloth. In the Bracken Paddock I could see Leonie and my father. He stalked her like a border collie tails a sheep, pressed her up against the pumpshed wall. I ate as I watched them.

Through the veil of branches below me I saw my mother come outside, barefoot in the garden, hands pushed out in the pockets of a long-stretched woollen cardigan she'd put on over her nightgown. Each day she looked more odd, her hair stuck out, no hat or parasol. She'd started burying things. She knelt and dug with her hands, got up and walked again. Back on her knees, she covered something up in among the hydrangeas and then went back inside.

I climbed down the trunk, careful not to be seen, dug it up to see what it was. A small silver box, with a scroll of script rolled up inside it. The writing on the parchment was funny looking, the letters inside out, nothing I could read.

"What's in your hand?" my father asked. He was standing over me. He seemed tall when I was kneeling.

"Found it in the garden," I told him. I didn't hear him come. He narrowed his eyes and took the silver from me.

"Do your skulking elsewhere," he said and disappeared.

My mother spent the remains of the morning locked in the bath, filling it deep even though we didn't have enough water. I went back up the tree.

Leonie came in for lunch, all cleaned up, short red hair and freckles, sat by my father like she'd been there fifteen years. My mother had tried to get herself together, but her cardigan was misbuttoned, her hair unravelled from its braid as she sat. She didn't seem to notice it collapsing about her shoulders. She used to look pretty when Dickie was around. Now her hair was the colour of string.

Her eyes locked onto the silver filigreed box. My father had placed it in the middle of the table between the shakers of salt and pepper. Stony-faced, he watched the tears that gathered in her eyes and ran across the tired skin around the high bones of her cheeks. She got up and left the room. She only had one shoe on.

She never ate at the table again. I left plates of porridge steaming on a bed tray at her door; she stayed in her room for a week.

My father comes in the kitchen from lighting the boiler so the water will be hot for my shower. He puts his hat on the table beside him. The porridge I'm cooking is thick enough to serve. I guide it from the pot into his plate with the wooden spoon until the Peter Rabbit pattern is all but covered.

"That was Mother's breakfast plate," I tell him. He doesn't seem fussed.

"Was it so bad that she was a Jew?" I ask him.

"She should have told me," he says.

My father leads a reluctant, sloe-eyed pony to the railing.

"Being that you're here, I thought you might help me do some feet," he says. I always hated trimming horses' hooves, he used to make me do them when I was young. I remember the ache in the pit of my back. America makes you soft, makes you want to pay to have things done.

"Pony looks like Push 'n' Jerk," he says as he ties it to a post outside the saddle room. He always called my pony Push 'n' Jerk. I called him Pope.

"This one has a mean eye," I say. Narrow eyes, showing too much white. Pope had big round eyes like a Welsh mountain pony.

I follow my father back to the corral, a leather headstall on his arm. He corners a big taffy-coloured horse and hands the rope to me. This one must be mine.

My father puts on a leather shoeing apron and gives me his second set of tools. He lifts his pony's foot up onto a steel tripod. There's no spare leather apron; he's left me a worn-down rasp. I want to go back up and change my pants, but he'll think that I've gone velvet.

"He's a bottler after stock, that horse," my father says, not looking up. A big lump of a station-bred horse, it leans all over me. It looks kind of useless. Its hoof in my hand is shaped like a sled from neglect. I pick up the pair of blunt toe clippers and get to work, careful not to cut the hoof back so far the white line shows. I hate it when they walk off tender.

My father's pony gets fidgety, doesn't want to keep its hoof stretched up in front of it. It flinches and the tripod flips, sends my father arse over elbow in the dirt. His fingers press instinctively over his bad eye to protect it.

"Jesus bloody wept," he says. He sits in the dirt in his farrier's apron, the rasp on the ground beside him. I kneel and wait for him to catch his wind. I don't know what to do. It's awkward when old people fall and pretend that they're not hurt.

"It wasn't my fault this time," I say. He pretends he doesn't know what I mean. I don't know whether to help him up or leave him sitting in the dust. His bad eye droops, crusted shut. As he shakes his face, I catch a glimpse of the pupil inside, mottled brown and bloodshot. It makes the other eye look big and sad.

One day he won't get up; I wonder if I'll be here. I offer him a hand and he looks at it before he takes it, as though it's not for him. His fingers are swollen and rough in mine.

"What did y'end up doing with Push 'n' Jerk?" he says. He struggles to his feet, he doesn't want me asking if he's hurt.

"I sold him for train fare."

He brushes his pants and turns to walk back to the house, leaving me to tend the tools and horses.

"I hope you got good money for 'im. He wasn't yours to sell."

I was eight. We worked in the dark. The cattle were wilder at night. My father lit the branding fire, poured in kerosene. Everything else was shapes and shadows. My mother said I was too young to be out so late in the yards, but the days were too hot to work in the sun.

I poked the long-handled brand in the bottom of the flames, waited for it to heat and go orange. My father cornered a calf, wrestled it in a headlock. As it bawled and struggled he stuck something down its mouth that I couldn't see, held the head up so it swallowed.

"What is it you put in them?" I asked him.

"A magnet," he said. He came to the fire to examine the brand.

"Cattle get hardware disease," he said. "Eat bits of wire and fencing staples." He told me they started fossicking for minerals when there wasn't any grass, how metals collected on the magnet on their insides that he sold it for scrap when he slaughtered. I wondered if he ever found silver or gold.

The branding iron glowed red and was ready. My father drove a steer down the chute and into the crush, then he belted it on the back with a length of pipe. It made a hollow sound.

He climbed the creosote rails, clothed in smoke from the fire. He nodded to me and I handed him up the brand.

His initials glowed orange in the dark as I lifted it to him. I held a rag around it, the handle was hot and it was heavy above my head.

"Make sure you don't drop it," he said. I concentrated on not being awkward. I held it so tight my knuckles were aching, passed it to him on my tiptoes.

He planted the letters in the rump, they sizzled and singed. The burnt hide smelt. At first it seemed cruel but then I got used to it. He passed the iron back. I had to keep it in the fire until the next steer was prodded into the crush.

We did seven and then eight. There weren't too many left. The smoke rested thick around my father as he stood above me on the fence. My eyes were watery and tired, it must have been almost midnight.

The ninth was in. The red kelpie dog made runs at its hocks and heels, my father pulled the wooden lever and the two-by-fours closed around its throat.

"This one's roguish," he said. "Stay still and let him settle."

It bellowed and stamped, the rope-tied railroad sleepers shook, it made the fences rattle. There was a banging and dust, the fence was breaking, my father fell towards me. I threw up my arm but the branding iron was still in my hand. I held on to it like he said, I didn't drop it. It met him in the eye like a boiling fist.

There wasn't ice, just goanna oil and gauzes he wrapped around his head. He wouldn't let my mother touch it. It was before the Flying Doctor Service. He wasn't taken to a doctor, he wouldn't go himself.

My mother said it wasn't my fault. My father never mentioned it. Then I heard them argue.

"Kid might as well have just come stuck it in my eye," he said. My mother tried to shush him.

"You oughtn't have him working in the dark."

"I won't be going near him," he said. I wasn't allowed in the yards again.

When the ruined eye was unbandaged, I wondered if there'd be part of the "D" or the "M" of his initials burnt into his face, but there wasn't. It was festered and strange, proud flesh forming, as if half his head wasn't his.

She made him a brown muslin patch, it had a strap along the bottom and the top. I never saw him use it. She wore it herself in a dust storm, tied it over her nose when she ran outside to cover the roses.

Dickie was coming. My mother had already written him. She said he would look after things, so my father could go to the Royal Eye and Ear in Melbourne. But my father never went. He didn't trust Dickie, not with the farm or my mother.

When Dickie called my father "Swivel Eye," I didn't tell him it was me who swivelled it.

“There’s a letter for ya, luv,” says the post office lady. I’m in town without my father for milk and mail. She plops it on the counter. “From Paris, France.” Stamps with Eiffel Towers, six of them together, they cover most of the front. The address is written in Callie’s untaught hand. I didn’t expect her writing back.

I sit on the bench outside the Maude post office and open the envelope, swiping at flies. She’s written on a brown paper bag torn open down the sides, her writing is sprawled in pencil on lines that angle down. “Dear Breaker Day,” it says. She doesn’t ask me how I am or mention she got my letter. She’s met a man called Nelson Pessoa, a famous rider from Brazil. She calls him “Neco.” Some say he’s the best in the world. He won the bronze medal in the Stockholm Olympics on a horse that wasn’t that good. He’s invited her to a horse show at a place called Puebla in Mexico. Riders flown in from Europe and America to compete on strange horses against the best of the locals. “All expenses paid,” she says.

“Neco thinks it’d be fun to have an Australian there. Get yourself a scarlet jacket with your flag sewn across the pocket.”

I notice a photo inside the envelope. A black-and-white Callie in one-piece bathers, the same plastic rain scarf on her head, bareback on the beach. The horse is cantering in hock-high water, the spray splashing up around her in white spots. A single rein on a Pelham bit, her hand pressed in the mane. Her legs are clamped around the horse, not back along its barrel but forward near the shoulder. I remember the colours through the lens, the horse that swam out to sea. Her green bathers, the steel-grey water.

On the back, in blotted ink, it says "Remember Rehoboth." It's her handwriting, but this time a horse that could swim. She must want to see me.

I read the letter a second time, then look at Callie's face in the photo, immovable against the horse and water, and I know that I will go. Just as there are days I hardly think of her at all.

I park the Vauxhall under the fig tree. I don't have the energy to get out of the car. I touch the letter in my pocket, watch my father as he walks towards me. His pants are ragged at the knees, like the trousers of a child. I have to tell him. I don't know why I thought it would be easy.

"Where have you been?" I ask him, as though he's the one who's up to something.

"Checking the cattle in Hindenburg," he says, leaning a hand against the roof of the car. Hindenburg isn't a paddock I remember.

"I started to call them after things that happened in the year they were fenced," he says. "Like Belafonte."

"Belafonte?"

"I heard this song called 'Island in the Sun'; they played it at the pub."

"Harry Belafonte's black," I tell him.

"I never saw a picture of him," he says. "Any mail?"

I get out of the car and pull the letter from my pocket, lean against the panel beside him. "I've been invited to ride at a thing in Puebla," I say as though it's a well-known place.

"Where's that?"

"Mexico."

He squints through the stunted cypress and into the lowering sun. "How will you get there from here?"

"Through Los Angeles. They said they'll pay my way. I haven't ridden for ages."

We go over and sit on the cemented arms of the veranda steps. He never pulls up on his trousers when he bends his legs to sit. His pale knees push through where his pants are worn. He looks deflated, like the wind's been taken from him.

"You can practise on old Nifty Dan," he says.

"I'll be all right."

The sun sets red around us like the desert's caught on fire. We watch it and listen to the evening birds.

"Is it the girl?" he asks.

I nod. "I'm meeting her there."

"It doesn't always work away from where it started," he says and scuffs a heel quite deep into the sand. The dog comes by and lays its head in the hole he's made.

"It's worth a shot," I say.

"I was getting used to you," he says as though he's talking to the dog.

I look down the drive to the sheds; an empty leather halter drapes from the fence. My mother could be walking back up to her roses with a trowel and a bucket of manure from the stockyards. But the garden is gone.

"Why did you put her in that bed?" I ask him.

For a moment he looks at the dog and doesn't answer.

"She'd gone peculiar," he says. "She still wanted to go to Europe but the War wasn't over. She'd wanted to go with Dickie Del Mar. Even he wouldn't take her."

I think of the body stuck up in the tree, it's almost as if

I imagined it. “Why did you make me think he was dead?”

“Because he was your father.” It catches me midbreath, to hear the words from him out loud, even though I already know them. Sitting on the steps in the late afternoon, all these years later. I look at him across from me, the furrows deep in his forehead, the sagging skin on his neck, the eye. I’ve carried him with me like a stone in my shoe.

I jump from my bedroom sill into the dirt, the way I did when I was small. A last white camellia rests in my open hand, plucked from its stem without leaves from the garden gone dry since she left it. I take her blue dress with me and walk barefoot across the paddocks in the dim-lit dawn, to the place I've been avoiding. The red sand is gritty under my feet, the grassy patches are dewy, the dockweed rips between my toes. On the bracken-covered rise by the billabong, the sagging chicken-wire fence keeps the cattle from her grave. There are shadows of horses on the Bracken Paddock hill. Sometimes I pretend I buried her myself, with flowers from her garden, the hole dug deep. But that's not how it was.

The fence is bent, pushed down by the chests of cattle leaning over to pick at the grass that's grown, dry paspalum that brushes the sandstone slab he chiselled with her first name and the year. It's not as strange as I've imagined it. I place the camellia gently on the stone, it bruises so easily. I kneel on the dress in the damp grass and touch the letters. "EMILY—1947." He engraved them himself.

I remember her wearing the dress, kneeling in the garden, shadows thrown from the veranda light. Her bare hands buried in the sand, moving a shrub like it couldn't wait until morning. I found her a trowel and her gardening gloves, put them on the cold ground beside her. She didn't seem interested in tools, she was elbows-deep in roots and dirt.

"It's the digging voice," she said, as though I'd know what she meant. I nodded like I understood, watched her for a while before I went inside.

Standing up, I shake the dress free of sand and grass stems. I'll wash it by hand and take it with me. I've been gathering bits of her to take away, I wonder if I can leave some things behind me.

I look up into the new dawn sky—small, white-tufted clouds. My mother called them mare's tails, a wisp of puce before morning. She taught me how to see colours. Streaks of red and yellow feathers on a passing lorikeet, when at first I only saw the green along its wings. Subtle colours. Pink and pale grey in a cockatoo feather, the cream of a gardenia, the browns where it was bruised. There was a rainbow once. She pointed out the shade lines in the sky. She didn't know the English for indigo. She knew violet, though. Red-blotted rims of her special yellow roses, blooming from dry sand, picked late and floated loose-petalled in shallow bowls in unexpected places, under her bed and in her bidet.

I walk back up the paddock with the dress under my arm, faded and far from its original colours. I spot a little knuckle in the grass, like one I'd collect and use for playing jacks. I reach down and pick it up. It's porous like coral, bleached very white against my hand. It's probably from a calf that died; I don't know what human knucklebones look like. I take it as a charm, I like the way it feels rough against my skin.

I see my father standing where the three gates meet. His squiffy eye looks worse in the half-light. I know he isn't well.

"I've been walking," I say, like it's normal to walk all night.

"To the grave?" he asks. I feel followed by him like I did as a child. He closes the gates behind me. I feel the knuckle in my palm and look at him. He tries to smile but his mouth has forgotten the shape.

I load up the Vauxhall, put my bags into the boot. It's early. Stripe-winged chuffs line the branches, magpies squawk from somewhere else. There's a mist above the ground, a beauty in the starkness you only notice when you're leaving.

My father drives me into Maude to catch the bus. We bump down the lane in silence. I try to remember the views, the shapes of the trees and the angular cattle, the smell of clothes dried hard in the sun.

The bus comes through from Broken Hill on Thursdays, sometime between seven and eight in the morning. We need to be there in case it's early. It'll be nighttime when I get into Melbourne, tomorrow I'll be on a plane. On Saturday I'll see Callie.

He waits with me on the post office bench. The morning breaks around us, the same time of day as when I rode out on the pony, when I left the first time.

"Dickie was good with horses and cattle," I say, almost as though it's a question.

"He made your mother laugh and stay up late," he says. "She used to laugh with me in Europe."

"And then?"

"She arrived with you," he says. "Never trust a man whose eyebrows meet, or a New Zealander."

"He wasn't from New Zealand."

"You don't have to be both of them to count," he says.

I listen for the rumble of the bus. It's almost seven o'clock. Darwin seems preoccupied, puts his hand against his cheek, as if remembering the make of his face before the eye, how he might have now looked windswept and interesting.

The bus grinds in and off the sealed road, dust engulfs us. He raises a hand to shield his eye. For a moment I can hardly see him, even though he's right beside me. I never patched the knees of his pants or got the garden going.

"Good luck," he says, "with the girl." He turns his head to look right at me, focusing. "It's a treacherous business."

PART THREE

"Nice bag of rocks, your horse," says Callie.

"Bloody thing jumped like a flying squirrel," I say. She hugs me hard but doesn't let it linger. I can tell she's glad to see me; it's been almost a year. She flops backwards onto her Mexican hotel bed. I put down my canvas bag of riding things and lean on the laminated table. There's a layer of scunge on everything.

Callie's room is on the third floor, looking out onto dusty hillsides, shanties made from cardboard and siding. My room is on the second floor, facing the other way. She's much the same except her hair is even shorter. Her legs are tanned, her ankle bones still the shape of apricots. Being around her makes me feel young as I was when I met her.

"I already sold the saddle," she says. Callie got the only good horse, even though she drew it from a hat. It looked like an ironing board but jumped like a stag. She won an unsuitable saddle and Mexican money. She counts her envelope of cash as she lies on the bed. She doesn't tell me how much there is. Her underarm is shaved; I can see it up her T-shirt sleeve. She didn't used to shave them.

I can't tell if her room is bigger than mine or if it's just that she doesn't have anything in it. The bed is pushed to the corner. There's no evidence of her except for a nail file and scissors on the bedside table. The maids don't straighten up during the day. You have to make your own bed here.

Callie lies on her side and begins to trim her nails. She files her thumbnail close to the quick. That's the way she's always done them, except now she uses a pale pink polish. She looks out the window.

"Up in those hills is where the life is," she says. I watch the daylight fading. The sky is purple, lights come on in streets that have them. If I smoked, I'd light a cigarette.

"We better get ready," I tell her. We're supposed to be at the farewell party by seven. It's already eight o'clock. Callie doesn't seem fussed that we'll be late.

"It'll just be the local odds and sods, speeches in Spanish. Puebla food," she says. Callie only eats carrots and salted pumpkin seeds. She has bags of them under the bed.

"And I don't have a dress," she says.

She gets up from the bed and takes off her T-shirt, pulls a beaded bedspread down from the wardrobe. She folds it in half and hitches it under her arms, over her breasts. It's orange and brown, faded near the bottom. She wonders about it in the strip of mirror on the wall.

"Fetching?" she asks me. "Like in that movie with the fire in Atlanta."

"If you take small steps, you can't see your sand shoes," I tell her.

She collapses back on the bed and looks at the ceiling.

"I have one with me," I say.

"A dress?" she says.

"It was my mother's."

Callie takes the bedspread off. She wears no bra, just

shorts and canvas running shoes. Her breasts are small, her stomach is flat. She is shorter than my mother, the shape of a twelve-year-old. She is twenty-one.

"Isn't that a little weird?" she asks.

I see myself in the dresser mirror, my mother's hooded eyes, the line of my nose. I am a little weird. I watch Callie reflected behind me. She lights a low candle in a saucer and gets in the bed with her back towards me. She lies there stiffly, like a pencil in a pocket.

The city seems quiet out through the open window. The candle shadows waft along the wall in the faint breeze. I sit in the dark where she can't see me. She stays deep in the bed looking into the corner of the room.

"How was your father?" she asks.

"He's not my real father." I say it matter-of-factly, as though it's of no great consequence. "My real one lives in Argentina." I talk that way when I'm with Callie, as if nothing really matters. I wish it wasn't that way.

"My father invented the confetti spreader," she says.

"What's that?"

"Exactly," she says.

The room is painted a dirt-stained yellow, it looks better in the flickery light. There's a faded colour photo of a church on the wall.

I get slowly into the bed behind her, as if she mightn't notice, and hold my arms around her. She feels like a little bony bird. Her shoulder blades point into me. I nestle my head between them and touch along the top of her underpants. Her skin is hot but she's not sweating. I pull her underpants down.

"Have you ever had someone inside you?" I ask her.

"Not since I was twelve."

"Who was that?"

"He was spreading his confetti," she says.

For a moment we are silent. I draw her closer and hug her tightly. She doesn't move.

"Are you okay?" I ask.

She nods. All I can see is the back of her neck; I can't see her face, but I know her eyes are open.

"Did you ever tell anyone?" I ask her.

"Nope," she says. Her shoulder blades stay sharp against me.

"When did it start?"

"I was nine, at first," she says. I try to imagine her at nine. It's like she's not much older now. Her narrow, curled-up shape clinging to the sheet.

"Where did you live?"

"Roanoke, Virginia. I slept in the bungalow, away from the house." She speaks deliberately, a finger pressed in the inside corner of her eye. She doesn't cry. "My not telling anyone made him proud," she says. The colour is gone from her voice.

I just hold her.

I wake up early. The sun comes streaming in. We never closed the curtains. Hazy air sits in the room. Boys in the street outside talk loudly. I lie on the covers in my undershorts. Callie kneels on the bed in her T-shirt, looking out the window. I feel awkward in the light of morning, I'm not sure what to say.

The room seems smaller than yesterday, stuffy, even with the window open. I get up and creep around like I don't have enough clothes on. We need to get outside.

I look at the church in the picture, take it off the wall and examine it. Foto Puebla is stamped in the corner in blue.

"It doesn't have a name," I say.

"If we take it with us, we can ask where it is," says Callie. It's as though we didn't talk about her father.

"Can I wear the dress?" she asks.

We walk along Avenida de las Pulgas, in the direction the man at the front desk pointed. There's something vaguely vaudeville about Callie in the dress. It's long on her and yet she doesn't look so out of place in Mexico. The town is all but empty, it's not yet eight o'clock. The dress is filmy, the faded colour of the sky.

We show people the photo as we go. They point us onward down nondescript streets, but the church is never there. We come to a plaza with a square cathedral, it's not our church at all. There are people going into it. It's Sunday. We walk past, we don't go inside.

Around the back, there's a stone bench beside a dried-up fountain with a Virgin Mary. Rusty water trickles down her face. You can light a candle for a peso. There are cigarette butts and bits of twigs in the bottom, insects drinking like they do in swamps.

"It must be holy water," says Callie.

She leaves a peso and takes two candles, puts one in her pocket.

"What was your mother's name?" she asks.

"Emily Neydhardt," I say. Callie lights a candle for her. I watch the wick as it takes. The air is so still the flame doesn't waver. She puts it on a spike in the candle stand and I put my arm around her, touch beside her mouth.

"We shouldn't kiss here," she says.

"When people get married they kiss in church," I say as I hold her to me.

"We're not in the church," she says. A button is loose on its thread, I feel it in my hand between her shoulders.

"Where's your father now?" I ask.

"His house burnt down," she says. "His hair and clothes burnt first."

Callie starts walking, away from the churchyard. A piece of the dress sheds free and wafts to the ground as she goes. I follow behind her and pick it up. The fabric's gone crisp in the sun, bits of it shed like feathers.

She takes the candle from her pocket, holds it up high in front of her, both hands clasped about it as if she's the local pope. She's joking but she doesn't smile.

"Hold the picture up," she says. A small girl watches us and smiles. She has a dead parrot in her plastic pram. Callie walks with long, low steps, a jerk with the knee then smooth and just above the ground to the tip of her stride, like a bagpipe player marching. A pale flower comes free from the hem, lands lightly in the dusty street. I bend down and pick it up, place it in my free hand. Callie motions me to keep the picture held up high. People watch us pass, but only for a moment, they don't seem to notice in particular. They have lots of rituals here; the women wear ragged, colourful dresses. The Americans look at us strangely as we enter the hotel.

Callie stands in front of the clouded mirror in the room, pulls what's left of the dress up over her head. It falls about her feet. I place my collection of faded pieces and fallen roses with it on the floor. She stands among them and looks at her body in the mirror. I look at it too. Her breasts, the way her stomach runs down to the line of her underpants. She holds her inverted hands around her neck, almost in a pose, her thumbs touch on her chest like a pendant. I let my trousers fall, my shirt slips down my arms. I stand naked beside her in the reflection. Our bodies are both thin, we look younger than we are. She only comes up to my chest even though I am not tall. We have well-tanned faces and arms, but her legs are brown from wearing shorts. She turns to look at me, we kneel and kiss, her neck and pelvis soften, she doesn't seem afraid. Her body doesn't usually bend unless she's on a horse. I catch bits of us moving in the mirror. We make love on my shirt and trousers, among the remnants of the dress.

Callie and I pull off the highway at Summerland, south of Santa Barbara. We've borrowed a Ford Prefect from a race-horse trainer she knows, from near the Los Angeles airport. She wants to drive up the coast to San Francisco.

I can see the place, the private polo field. I stop on the verge beside the service road. A man long-reins a young horse, driving it from behind. I roll down the window and watch.

He flaps a rein softly on its side, sends the horse forward at a trot, turns it in a big figure eight. The man glides along behind, like he's dancing in the grass. He wears a wide-brimmed hat with a tie under his chin. He's narrow at the waist, the slim-fit trousers. "That's him," I tell Callie. I can't see his face, but I know it's Dickie Del Mar.

"Better than your average Argentinian," she says. She's not a snob about anything, except horses.

We walk down to the field towards him as he takes a cube of sugar from his pocket and feeds the horse with an open hand, like he taught me as a boy. As we get closer, he looks up. His face is lined, his eyebrows are bushy and greying, handsome in the shadow of his hat. He still has his hair, the cleft in his chin, but his shoulders are slightly stooped. I wonder if I'll look like him when I'm older.

"Nice little horse," I say.

He waits for me to say something else, but we just look at each other. The breeze has stopped. He wipes the sweat from around his eyes with the back of his sleeve and looks at me again. A twitch in his jaw that connects down the side of his neck.

"You're Emily's Day," he says, hardly a trace of the accent.

I nod. He moves to shake my hand but doesn't look directly at me. His hold is soft, his fingers smooth for a man who's spent his time outdoors. He's careful around me, not sure why I've come.

"This is Callie," I say. "She's how I found you."

"Through Federico Castaing," she says. He smiles; he knows who that is. A tooth is missing from the side of his mouth.

"We came from an invitational show in Mexico," she says. "He was riding for Argentina."

Dickie takes off his hat and shapes it, pushes at his hair. The youngster stands patiently, the reins in coils on the ground. The groom brings his next horse out.

"Let me jump on this one before it gets dark," he says. He bunks up, rides down the track at a comfortable canter. I should have called to give him warning. I hope he doesn't leave.

"He shakes hands like a woman," says Callie.

"Doesn't mean he's not my father," I say.

Callie's asleep in the car. She'd rather be driving north, she wanted to be in Carmel by morning. I wait for Dickie in the shade of a tree. A breeze comes in from the water. He rides back to the barn from another direction. He wants to walk with me down to the ocean. He thinks we should be alone.

"Sometimes there are dolphins," he says.

The track is steep and narrow. He's sure-footed, moves quite fast, even though the sand is uncertain. The beach is empty, the sun is going down.

"I heard you ran away when your mother died," he says.

He takes off his paddock boots, rolls up the bottoms of his trousers. He's not wearing socks. He has long, dark feet, like people who walk on the sand.

"You shouldn't have left," I say.

Dickie looks out to sea. "Would you like a swim?"

He doesn't wait for an answer, strips down to nothing and leaves his clothes on the beach. I still have my shoes on. He lopes to the edge and wades through the shallows, slows up as the water gets deeper. His body is dark, taut like a long-distance runner's. Elastic strokes, fingers together, his hands swoop through the water on angles, his shoulders reaching, brushing past his ears. I watch the easy rhythm of his feet, imagine him making love to my mother. If I could swim I would join him.

"Well?" says Callie. She's snuck up behind me. It's getting cold, I can see her nipples through her T-shirt. "Do I call you Day Del Mar?"

"He keeps going off in different directions," I say.

Dickie emerges from under a wave, wipes the water from his eyes. When he sees Callie, he seems self-conscious.

I take his clothes down to him. Callie comes with me to look.

He puts on shorts and dries himself on his undershirt.

"Did you marry my mother?" I ask him. He squints and shakes his head. I take the photo from my jacket pocket; I keep it in a plastic wrapper. He dries his hands so he can hold it.

"I took that," he says, "after I met her in Vienna. She got all dressed up and stood in the snow. The day she was married it rained, she said nobody took any pictures."

He gives it back to me. I look at her, standing alone by the fountain. "Was she happy or sad?" I ask.

"She was beautiful."

His eyes look tired. I wish I had a copy he could keep. "She took her marriage seriously," he says. "It was a different time."

Dickie asks us to wait, says he's going to take us to dinner, a Mexican place in Montecito.

"We've just been to Mexico," says Callie. She hates Mexican food, but Dickie doesn't hear her.

He comes back showered and changed, his hair combed wet across his head. He wears a collarless shirt, open down the front; his chest is bare and flat. The shirt is white and almost see-through. He has on cigarette-leg pants.

Callie wants to drive his car. He doesn't seem to mind. It's a burgundy Buick with fins. He gets in the front beside her. She pretends she doesn't like him, but I know that she's intrigued.

"How far's San Francisco?" she asks him as she turns onto the highway. She's low behind the wheel, she needs a box to sit on.

"Eight hours up the coast," he says.

"We could be there by morning," she says. I wonder what happened to Carmel.

The waiter walks with one hand out behind him as though he's leading a dog. Dickie seems to know him. He orders food in Spanish, something that's not on the menu. They bring him a carafe of white wine; he tastes a sample before they fill the glass. Callie and I order chicken burritos, no beans, and orange juice. Neither of us drinks.

"Is Darwin still alive?" asks Dickie.

"He's out there on his own," I say. "He looks a bit decrepit." I talk about him as though he's someone else's favourite horse. It feels mean to have said it; I know that he's not well. "The eye still bothers him," I say. Dickie leans back in his chair, remembering.

"What happened to his eye?" asks Callie.

Dickie and I look at each other, wait for the other to answer.

"An accident," he says.

"I put a red-hot poker in it," I say.

"You were only eight years old," he says; he knew all along it was me who'd done it. Callie seems impressed.

The food arrives. Pale, wrapped-up lumps on a plate for Callie and me. Dickie's comes out steaming, shrimp and peppers and strips of steak on a flat iron pan. Callie starts eating, her napkin still in its ring on the table. Dickie tucks his in his shirt, takes thin tortilla bread and wraps the food himself, pleating the corners neatly like sheets on a hospital bed. He spoons red and white sauces on top.

"Did you know her family?" I ask him.

"I met her parents. In Vienna," he says. "They didn't survive the War."

"They were Jewish, weren't they?"

"Her mother was," he says. "How do you know that?"

"I found her book of prayer. I saw her in the dark with candles." I pick at the edge of my burrito, trying not to remember.

"Do you have parents?" I ask him.

"My mother lived in La Plata, near Buenos Aires," he says. "She didn't know about you." I look up at the coloured bunting that loops along the wall. Callie kicks me under the table. She heard him say it too.

Dickie orders dessert for us all, an assortment of sugary flans on a tray.

"My father's dead," says Callie.

"I'm sorry," says Dickie.

"It was for the best," she says.

A man comes by dressed up in a sombrero and a ruffle-fronted shirt, wants to play his guitar. Callie rolls her eyes as Dickie speaks more Spanish. The man strums and begins to sing.

"A song for your mother," Dickie says to me. "The clouds go through the sky, the fish through the water." He translates each line in a serious whisper. "The gold is under the ground, *y el amor está en las enaguas*, and love is in the petticoats." He pauses, wistful. "I used to sing that to her."

"I only remember the tango," I say. "In the agapanthus."

I look down at my plate, remember my mother watching him dance. I stem the tears as they well.

"She called them 'Agatha's Pants,'" says Dickie, pretending not to see.

"How come you left?" Callie asks him.

"Every day she was stranger. She wanted to go back to Vienna, but it wasn't safe for her." He answers Callie, but he's talking to me. "Darwin was always watching, he never seemed to sleep. He made me help him with the muster. When we had the cattle herded, he started to swing his rifle around, said I had to leave or he'd get even."

"He got even," I say. "He didn't let her out of the house, then he locked her up with a thing in her mouth, a bed with special sides. Seven weeks and she suffocated."

"Day still has some pieces of her dress," says Callie.

Dickie wrings his napkin between his hands, looks into his drink.

Whenever I see a telephone in a rich person's house I want to sneak a call to somewhere far away. Dickie Del Mar has his phone in a cubicle inside the front door, like in the foyer of an expensive hotel. It's wallpapered with covers from the *New Yorker*.

I watch him and Callie in the living room at the end of the hall, under the light of a tall standard lamp, talking about horses and breeding and Argentina. He's lit her up a dark cigarette. Callie just holds it. She doesn't put it near her mouth.

I pull the phone room door behind me, dial the long-distance operator and whisper the run of numbers. Dickie shouldn't mind, I haven't been expensive. It's not like he put me through college. Darwin's line is not connected. I ask her to try Leonie's number at the pub. Leonie answers the phone in the bar; I can hear the din of drinking, the loud Australian laughter. When she realises it's me she starts talking before I say why I've called. I want to tell her how I uncovered Dickie Del Mar.

"Darwin's crook," she says. "He had some sort of a stroke." She talks quickly as if she's saving me money. "I got him on a mattress in the back of the ute and drove him to Deniliquin."

"How is he now?"

"Not so good," she says. "Why are you whispering?"

Someone shouts Leonie's name from the bar. "I gotta go," she says, "there's a whole crowd here. Come if you want to."

I replace the handpiece quietly and stand in the dark. Dickie and Callie are still talking. She sits on the edge of the couch, he's in a dark leather chair. His features haven't softened with age. He must be over fifty. It's hard to tell what he's thinking by his expression, he always looks slightly amused. Callie watches her cigarette smoke as it rises faintly from the tip. I walk outside to be on my own.

I imagine Darwin's body bumping along Muddy Gates Lane on the bed of a truck, the sun on his face. His dried-up tongue in his throat, his eye, Leonie looking back through the rearview mirror, taking him to the hospital.

Dickie's garden is pretty at night, there are crickets. I climb a good way up a loose-barked eucalyptus and straddle a limb, let my legs dangle. I look out over the Pacific and wonder what it would be like to live here.

Callie comes out to see where I am. She whistles with two fingers, calls me up like a dog.

"I'm here," I say from above her.

She looks up at my feet. "Should we call the fire brigade?" she asks.

"Why? Did you light one?"

The waves break on the beach at the bottom of the cliffs, they sound like traffic passing on a highway.

"Darwin's dying," I tell her.

"Did he call to tell you?" she asks. She knows what I've been up to.

I notice Dickie standing in the doorway, the foyer light behind him. I can see his shape but not the features of his face as I watch him through the leaves. Callie doesn't see him there.

"Maybe Dickie'll buy us airplane tickets," she says. "After all, he is your father."

"Who?" I ask, unsure which one she means.

"Dickie," she says.

I imagine Darwin on a narrow hospital bed, hooked up with tubes and drips. I look over at Dickie behind the screen door.

"Perhaps Dickie'd like to come with us?" I say. The tip of his cigarette goes orange as he puts it to his mouth. "He could see where my mother is buried."

"If he was so excited about your mother he wouldn't have left her there," says Callie.

"I loved his mother," says Dickie from the doorway. He comes down the steps onto the lawn, picks up a sprig that fell when I was climbing, swats Callie lightly on the back.

"Then take us back there," I say.

~

"If we crash in the water," says Callie, "we should try and get a lifeboat to ourselves." She has the inflatable vest out from under the seat, she's checking the clasps and attachments. "I think we'd have a better chance," she says.

I look out the window of the plane and into the darkness. If people heard they'd think she was serious.

"You really should learn to swim," she says.

"Perhaps you'll teach me from the raft," I say. I imagine Callie floating in a lifeboat, me learning to swim alongside. The fuselage sinking in the distance.

"Dickie swims like an eel," she says.

"Why an eel?"

"The way they swim," she says.

Hardly anyone sits near us, those who do are asleep. Callie doesn't sleep on planes. She says she's too excited.

"You only came because he's paying," I say.

"That's not altogether true," she says. "You're here too." I lean over and kiss her but she tries to read her magazine around my face. "You kiss too hard," she whispers.

"What do you mean?"

"Too much mouth and tongue," she says.

"What about in Mexico?" I say.

"It was different there," she says. "I felt like I was someone else."

When I wake up Callie's gone. We still haven't flown into daylight. I get up and go to the bathroom and brush my teeth. Through the crack in the curtain I see her kneeling in the aisle. She's talking to Dickie. He has a more expensive ticket than the ones he bought for us. He got them in Santa Barbara, said he had a travel agent. It was generous and I'm glad he did it but I'm uncertain why he came. I didn't think he'd want to be reminded of the past. The prospect of him and Darwin unnerves me, and what Callie will think of the farm, the way it's so primitive there.

I open the curtain to join them but the hostess catches me. "You can't both be up there at once," she says. "Wait until your sister comes back."

I return to my seat and read. Dickie has more to say to Callie. When he talks to me it's as though he's afraid to be reminded of the things we have in common.

Callie brings me back a glass of water.

"How come you said you were my sister?"

"I didn't," she says. "I said Dickie was my father."

"Why?"

"So they'd let me up to see him," she says. The things I like about her most are sometimes those I like the least.

"What did you two talk about?" I ask. She's filing her nails, they're already short.

"How he was poor and now he's rich."

"How did he get rich?"

"He hasn't told me yet," she says.

There's weather coming into Papeete, the rain looks black against the window, pelting silently. We have to stop to refuel. The lights on the landing track are few and barely visible, even though we're close to the ground. A sudden windshift has one wing swinging up, people shriek and glasses tumble. I jam my knees and grab Callie's arm. Her eyes go big and she smiles like this is pretty good, but her hand is tight on mine as though it's all she has. A revving of engines makes the windows shudder; a camera tripod goes end over end in the aisle as the plane drags upwards, righted, the landing aborted.

"Touch and go," says Callie as she looks out into the night. "I saw palm trees," she says. I imagine Dickie sitting rigid up in the front, finishing off his Johnny Walker.

As we come in a second time, everyone is silent, even Callie. I watch a woman praying, the quiver of her lips, her thumbs to her mouth, a rosary bound in her fingers. I stare open eyed at the tartan pattern on the seat back in front of me, think of my mother murmuring prayers, sitting among candles on the dark, bare boards. I breathe again as the wheels touch the tarmac, relief in the screech of the landing gear.

"I've never been to the tropics," Callie says calmly.

"It's okay to be afraid," I say.

Out of Auckland, it's still before dawn. The plane rattles up into the air. Callie takes a photo out the window but you can't see much.

"What's Australia going to be like?" she asks.

"A big farm with flies."

"Is it beautiful?"

"In a bleak sort of way. Heat and open spaces sound attractive, until that's all there is."

"Are there waterfalls?" she asks. "A beach?"

"Not where we're going," I say. I don't tell her the desert was once the floor of an ocean.

The filtering light of the morning begins to appear above an orange rim of cloud. I wait for the mass of land on the horizon, hints of green along the edges, the sun already up and over it.

There's a breathing apparatus on Darwin's mouth, a hint of recognition in his eye. He's propped up on pillows. A tube goes into his out-turned arm, just below his birthmark. I watch his freckly fingers move, not much more than a lifting of their tips from the sheet. I can't tell if it's an effort to acknowledge me or a tap of impatience.

The room is so hot it's hard to breathe. There's a high window with a view of the sky, but it's not the sort that opens. An electric cooler sits on a bench and fans across him. Each time it passes, a few strings of his hair rise up from the sweat on his scalp and the curtain beside him billows. The grind of the fan with the buzz of the blowflies makes a dull, annoying sound. There are no cards or flowers.

"Leonie told me," I say.

He nods with special effort so I know he understands. His bad eye is covered with a puffy white patch. The good eye is bloodshot, silent and uneasy. I wonder if he wants to live or die.

"My friend Callie came with me," I say. "The one I went to meet in Mexico." I don't mention Dickie Del Mar, the unexpected guest. I pull a chair over, closer to the bed.

"Do you want to stay here?" I ask him.

He tries to respond, to spit the thing from his mouth,

but it stays where it is. He scrunches his fingers into a weak fist and then his fingertips extend.

Leonie walks in with Darwin's brindle dog following. It lies down beside the bed like it's visited before. I've never seen a dog in a hospital. Leonie wears a green skirt, her hair pulled back. Darwin strains to see her.

"You're all dolled up," I say. I shepherd her out into the corridor to talk.

"You said you had American friends," she says.

"They're out getting food. Americans get tricky if you don't keep them fed." I don't know why I've said it, Callie goes for days without eating and Dickie isn't from there.

"Darwin wants to go home," I say.

"He's talking?" she asks.

"We can't just leave him here," I say.

"I'm buggered if I can look after him," she whispers too loudly. I stamp at a square of linoleum that's buckled in the heat.

"I could do it for a week. See how it goes."

"He might stay alive for years," she says.

"I'd rather be home than here."

Darwin gets rolled out into the sun on a squeaking gurney. They've taken him off the oxygen. Leonie in her skirt and the brindle dog follow. I set up the mattress in the back of her utility truck. It smells like a mattress that others have died on.

The matron says he only needs the breathing mask if no one's around. He can't attach it himself. "If he needs it," she says, "he'll be wheezing or panicked."

We slide him from the gurney. The hospital people aren't much help. They don't like it when relatives appear from nowhere and make their own arrangements. I take a hold under his arms, my thumbs fit deep into the grooves between his shoulder bones. Leonie takes his legs. We push and pull him, careful as we can.

"You're heavy," I tell him. The ties in the front of his hospital smock pull open. I cover him up with a sheet. The dog jumps up and carefully steps around him, puts its head out the side. Leonie ropes the suitcases onto the tailboard. I stay in the back to travel with him and the cylinders of oxygen. Darwin looks pale outside.

"Are you alright?" I ask him.

I pull the sheet up to shade his face, but he shakes his head slightly. He doesn't want to be covered.

The road to Maude is straight as a die. I sit on the spare

wheel in the back, Darwin dozes on the mattress. I move so my shadow covers his face, put my hand close to his nostrils, feel his breath on my fingers.

He sleeps despite the noise of the motor and the hiss of the tyres on the thin strip of tar. Loose bits of straw fly up around us from the tray of the ute. The wind sweeps the face of his black and white dog so it looks like it's smiling.

The others all sit in the front: Leonie and Callie and Dickie Del Mar. I can't see their faces, just the backs of their heads through the dirty glass. I never imagined the three of them together. Callie is in the middle, straddling the hump on the floor. Her hair is cut irregular and short across the back; she trims it herself so it ends up at angles. Leonie drives. I can already tell she doesn't like Callie by the way she leans against the door away from her. Dickie puts his narrow brown arm along the back of the seat behind her. I slap the roof of the cab and Callie turns to see me. I wipe the dust from the window. She twists her mouth as she forces the sliding part of the glass.

"Everything okay?" she asks.

"Do you have enough room? You can sit back here if you like."

Dickie's leathery arm rests like a reptile between us, his slender fingers clasp the width of the seat top. He looks out his side, off into the spinifex.

"I'm fine," she says. She calls to the dog but the dog ignores her. Now that the window's open the others don't speak. No one wants Darwin to know about Dickie. I pick up a rusted wrench from beside me and play with the adjustment, watch Dickie's loose khaki pant leg and wonder if he wants to press his leg against Callie's jeans. I remember how he brushed against my mother's leg, their feet as tight as magnets.

I throw the wrench out the back of the ute, watch it spin up through the air then clang on the road behind us. A semitrailer sounds its horn as it comes from the other direction, its iron crates rattling. Jammed-up sheep bulge through the slats on the side, dust storms up as its wheels leave the bitumen. Dickie rolls his window up. I put the oxygen fitting over Darwin's nose and mouth, paste down the tape that's come loose from the patch on his eye.

Callie turns and kneels back around on the seat, puts her head through the open bit of the window. "How's Darwin doing?" she asks.

"He's keeping to himself," I say.

She calls to the dog again. "He must be deaf," she says. It bares its teeth to the wind. I wave the flies from around Darwin's mouth. "Border collies are my favourites," she says, "except they run around in circles."

As we turn into Muddy Gates Lane the dust rises behind us like billowing linen. Leonie slows down to a crawl as we loll in and out of the ruts. I steady the oxygen barrel. Callie looks down the track.

"Is this it?" she asks.

"We still have a mile to go."

"There aren't any signs," she says.

"Signs of what?" I ask.

She looks at me squarely. "Life," she says. She scans the

salt grass flats, squints as if she must be missing something.

I shade my eyes as though I can see what she doesn't, but there's nothing in particular, save anthills, some of them higher than horses, rising up from the plain. We pass the occasional boxgum growing this way or that to avoid the harshness. Rangy cattle seek shade. Outbreaks of hore-hound are the only traces of green.

"If you have to cross a distance there should be some-thing on the other side," says Callie.

"What were you expecting?" I ask.

"I just came to be with you," she says.

"Then why aren't you sitting back here?"

I push the veranda bench against the wall, back into the shade. "In there's where my mother died." I motion through the window. Callie pokes at the fly-wire where it's rusted through. The pane is greyed with webs, it's dark inside. The shape of the bed is visible.

Dickie's made a jug of Pimm's with ginger ale and spears of wild mint he picked from around the underground tank. He brings it out on a tray, sets it down on the cemented arm of the steps and pours us both a glass. He's forgotten we don't drink.

He fills a taller glass for himself, stands at the bottom of the steps with his face in the air. Callie and I sit on the bench and look out in the direction of the road. Dickie pours again and takes his second drink for a walk. He walks like he doesn't want to get dirty, crouches down at the stubble of the dahlia bed, then moves on. He props up the fallen trellis where the black-eyed Susan grew among the climbing roses.

"Dickie's gone quiet," says Callie.

I empty my drink on a dead geranium by the steps.

"This used to all be lawn," I say. "There were agapanthuses down where he's standing."

Callie sips her drink. I've never seen her drink before. I lean back into the shade and watch her, the sun is hot all over the place. She's got a clip in her hair.

"We used to play music outside," I say. "Dickie brought a gramophone for my mother."

I fish a bee from the slice of lemon floating in Dickie's jug of Pimm's.

"Leonie said your mother lost her marbles," says Callie, "said she should have been in hospital."

"Darwin kept her home," I say.

One end of the clothesline, broken at the knot, still hangs from the veranda post just near me. There's an old wooden peg in the dirt.

"When did you start drinking?" I ask her.

"When I was breast-fed," she says and we laugh.

Dickie walks up to the far end of the veranda and puts his glass on the edge. He takes off his leather sandals and carries them in one hand. He treads barefoot towards Darwin's bedroom window, each step careful so the boards don't creak. He pokes his neck and chin, looks in from the side.

"What's he afraid of?" asks Callie.

"They don't get on that well," I say.

The brindle dog growls loudly from inside Darwin's room, then barks. Dickie withdraws, backs off the boards and onto the dirt. He grabs his empty glass and carries his sandals.

"Was that Darwin or the dog?" says Callie.

Dickie sits down on the bench beside me, folds his legs. He smiles, but he doesn't think it's funny. He leans down to refill his glass from the jug, sets it up on the bluestone sill. Callie and I watch the way he moves, it's languid and graceful, and foreign. He has long wrists. He raises his hand to shade his eyes, squints through the fly-wire window and into the locked-up room.

"That's the bed," I say without turning around to look in with him. He studies it, his fingers on his chin. I look at his dusty brown feet. I wonder if he knew the bed had sides.

Callie had another Pimm's and disappeared. She comes in to dinner, dressed up as my mother; she's been rummaging in the trunks.

"You found the linen closet," I say.

An old-fashioned winter slip, heavy linen straps on the shoulders, embroidery on the hem. It hangs long on her; she thinks that it's another dress. She's drunk.

"I was looking for the gramophone," she says.

Dickie looks around from the sink. He's washing plates so they'll be clean enough to eat from. He begins to smile but stops when he sees what she's wearing. His eyes linger on her for a second, as if he's remembering. It makes Callie awkward. She smiles at him, it's not her usual smile. She fingers an oblong brooch. Dickie picks up a plate he's already dried, puts it back in the water.

Callie has on navy shoes, they're long for her feet. A pair my mother would have worn when she still used stockings; when she still wore shoes. Callie's a little unsteady on them. She sees me looking down.

"They're a bit big," she says.

She sits down on a kitchen chair, slowly, as though someone might be sitting there already. She clasps her hands on the place mat in front of her; she's wearing small white gloves.

"What's for dinner?" she asks.

Dickie has a pot on the electric stove. I have one on the Aga. I'm warming a tin of applesauce for Darwin.

"Spaghetti Bolognese, sans spaghetti, mit toast," says Dickie. He has on black pants and a loose white shirt; he seems to have cut his hair and wetted it down. I'm the only one not dressed for dinner.

"Would you like a drink to start with?" he says to Callie.

She shakes her head. "I think I've had enough." She smiles to herself, as though she's kept it a secret. She smells of mothballs and lavender sachets.

"Why are you wearing my mother's underwear?"

"I had to find something," she said, "we're dining with Dickie Del Mar." She looks down at herself in the chair. "I thought it was a dress."

She fingers the laces that gather at the side.

"They're for underneath," says Dickie. He puts plates on the table as I open the can of applesauce, put it with a spoon on a wooden drinks tray, pour a glass of milk for Darwin.

"My mother didn't wear petticoats," I say.

"She had on that one," Dickie says, "under the wedding dress."

I remember his song about love among the petticoats. "She didn't wear it out here," I say.

"Nod if you're ready to breathe on your own," I say. There's sweat on Darwin's forehead. I hope it's the heat and not fever. I shouldn't have warmed up the food. I remove the tube slowly from his throat. I'm getting better at it. The canker sores are still inside his lips. It's strange being so close to his face, right near the patch on his eye. I wonder why they covered it.

"I think your eye should have some air," I say.

I pull the tapes off slowly, they leave flat places in the creases on his temple. The eye is worse than I remember, blighted and swollen, there's pus in the corners. I'm not sure I can look at it and feed him applesauce. I tape it back. "It's fine," I say. He knows that it isn't.

"Apple custard," I say. "Custard" sounds better than "sauce." I guide a spoonful to his mouth, put the tip inside. "I warmed it, but it's not hot." It goes down better than before, even though I can't see him swallow. I wonder if he's hungry.

He pushes his hand against my pants. I look at his face but his fingers keep jostling, his head doesn't move. He's making shapes on the sheets, trying to draw something, but his hands are big, they get in the way. I kneel beside him so I can see; he's tracing letters.

An "F" then an "A," an "R," and an "M." It takes such an

effort; his fingers go still. He's worried about the animals.

"I'm keeping an eye on things," I say. I can hear a calf outside, pulling at grass in the garden. He probably hears it too, thinks fences are down, cattle are out on the road. He looks up at the ceiling. His face is like a gravel road, rutted and uneven, one eye always open, unblinking like a puddle, the other always closed. Sometimes when I come into the room I think he's dead.

I look into the empty fireplace, into the ashes of logs he chopped on nights he couldn't sleep. I finish the apple-sauce from the tin, drink the rest of the milk, listen to his uneven breathing. I get up and force the window open to give him some air.

There's music playing faintly in the dark. I look around the unlit garden. Callie and Dickie are dancing, her head to the side pressed into his low-buttoned shirt. He hops the track the wheelbarrow made. Callie's taken off her shoes and gloves. The winter slip clings around her, against his legs; her feet are up on his, hooked through the straps on his sandals. They glide along where the cooch grass was. I smell the strange woody scent of the dark cigarette that floats in his free hand. The record crackles as it turns, Callie's head goes upside down when he dips her. Dickie sweeps his drink up in his cigarette hand as they swoop past the steps, a swig for himself and what's left for Callie. He tips the glass to her open face, and I remember how it was, the sweat from his chest on the silk of his shirt, the tan on the leather of his neck. They think they're alone.

A dryness collects in my mouth. I want to say something so they'll stop, but I just watch them. Darwin scrapes at the sheets, not just his fingers but the heels of his hands, an empty sound from his glaucous throat. He tries to rear up, to see if it's real. The scratchy tango, the cigarette smell that wafts in the window. He wants to rise up but he can hardly move. Words are coming, from deep inside him, husky, barely audible. He sounds like a deaf person speaking. "Don't let them dance," he hisses.

I call out Callie's name, down into the paddocks. They stop, sudden in the wheelbarrow tracks, still as a sculpture with the night dripping off them. Callie looks up but she can't see me. Dickie doesn't take his eyes from her. He places Callie's hand back on his shoulder, glides her away into the shadows of the cypress, around the corner of the house, the pale winter slip floating through the dark like a witness.

I raise the kerosene lamp in my hand to light their faces as I walk towards them. Dickie stubs his cigarette on the sole of his sandal, drills it into the leather as if it won't go out. He looks like he's been interrupted. Callie's not sure how close to stand, she smiles but doesn't speak. Her hair is wet, her feet are bare, the slip is damp and askew. Her cheeks are red from drinking.

"We were only dancing," she says.

"Come inside," I tell her. Moths come down from the dark and hover about the lamp. She follows me up the path, walks down the hall behind me.

"We can talk in here," I say. I unlock the door with the key I found on Darwin's mantelpiece. The bed looks smaller than my memory of it, the room is unlit and stuffy, shadowy in the light from the lantern, the air from all those years.

"I'm going to ask him to go back to America," I say.

"I'd be bored if he wasn't here."

"Then you should go with him," I say.

She leans against the rail of the rusted bed, scratches a bite on her arm until it bleeds. She licks her finger and smears it. She doesn't know what she wants.

"What happens if Darwin gets better?" she asks.

Dickie's out through the window, the gramophone under his arm. He looks beaky side-on, older in the dark on his own.

"I don't want to stay here," says Callie.

"Then don't."

There's a noise in Darwin's room, a dull thump on the boards. I look in the door and see Dickie bent over, picking up flowers and putting them back in the jar, blotting spilt water with his hanky.

"I'm sorry," he says, as much to the floor as to anyone. He gets up, reaches the chair for support. He's drunker than I've seen him, a cigarette still in one hand. I watch in case he burns things. Darwin watches him too.

Dickie takes his wine glass from the mantel, leans on the window ledge and looks out into the night. I crouch against the wardrobe, inside the door where he won't see me.

"I thought you'd look after Emily," he says to Darwin without looking around from the window. The words drag from his throat.

Darwin's uncovered eye is burnished in the light of the bedside lamp.

"I wouldn't have left if I'd known you'd keep her in that bed," says Dickie. He takes a halfhearted draw from his limp cigarette. "She wanted the baby. I didn't," he says, more to himself. "I didn't want a wife and child. She was already married to you."

Darwin's good eye closes slightly. Mosquitoes hum to rest on his face. He can't move to swat them.

Dickie tips some ash on the floor and looks at the jar

of wilting flowers. "I left her in Vienna when she was twelve weeks pregnant," he says. He rests his angular hip against the chair. I only see a little of myself in him, I'm slender but not as tall or dark complexioned.

"She didn't know what she was coming to," he says. He drains what's left of his drink. "You told her it was beautiful here." He looks at Darwin, just for a second, and then back out the window.

"When I came out here, it was mostly to avoid the War," he says. He puts his glass against his cheek. "You were right not to let her go back, she couldn't just travel to Europe."

I didn't know he left us here mostly of his own accord, that he didn't take much convincing. I remember the body strung up on the river. It would have been better if it were his.

"You should have sent her to an institution," he says to Darwin. "She might still be alive." I get up from the floor, I've heard enough. Dickie's a man of excuses.

"She wasn't likely to live," I say, "men like you to look after her." I say it more loudly than I mean to.

Callie comes up the hall from the living room, her eyes all bleary from sleep. "What's going on?" she asks. "Are your fathers fighting over you?" She still smells of Bitters and Pimm's.

Dickie stands straight when he sees her. "Darwin and I were just talking," he says before I can speak. He runs his hand through his hair, composing himself.

"Darwin didn't say much." I say it sarcastically.

"I thought you said they were enemies," Callie says to me.

"They're enemies of themselves, not each other," I say.

Dickie's cooking eggs at eleven P.M., scrambled with mint from the tank. He pours in Tabasco and a nip of his drink. The kitchen smells vaguely of liquor. Callie's asleep on the couch. I can see her through the door to the sitting room. The linen slip has ridden up high on her legs. I catch Dickie watching her; he's too drunk to be subtle.

I play patience on the kitchen table with a furry deck of cards. The pack is so old it's hard to shuffle. I'm afraid to go to bed. They won't be alone if I'm around.

He serves himself a plate of salmon-coloured mush from the pan. Scrambled eggs must be what drunk people eat at midnight. He sits himself down at the end of the table, puts a forkful to his mouth. He doesn't offer me any. He swings another glance at Callie. He can't help himself.

"I wonder what I'd be like if I'd grown up with you," I say. I lay out cards, pretend I'm interested in what comes up.

"Maybe you'd enjoy things more," he says. He pours himself a tumbler of Darwin's stout. He's less fussy about his drinks as the night wears on. Callie doesn't move in her sleep. "You might have learnt how to make her happy," he says, motioning at Callie.

The way he says it makes my skin feel different, like prickly heat. I grab the table, shove it at him, my fingers tight as teeth around the edge. It slides quick and definite, hits him midchest, flips him from his chair, scrambled eggs and broken glass beside him on the brown linoleum floor.

He gets up, rubs his elbow, tucks in his white silk shirt. He doesn't seem surprised. He brushes past Callie who's awake and up in the doorway. The touch of his forearm against her is so slight I can't tell if it's real. He doesn't look back as he walks up the hall.

I bend down and pick up bits of my mother's plate. Callie gets a sponge from the sink, she doesn't ask what happened.

"Did you tell Dickie we don't make love?" I ask her. She soaks up his drink from the floor but misses most of it.

"I said we did once," she says. "In Mexico. He said most men don't know how." She gets up and wrings out the sponge in the basin. I pick up the playing cards. Some of them tear from being wet.

"If he leaves will you go with him?" I ask.

"Did you ask him to go?"

I hate it when she answers with a question. "Not yet," I say. I look down at the floor, crouched on all fours. Callie looks out the window, but there's nothing to see. She's different when she's drunk, maudlin, like she doesn't care at all. We're usually the two who haven't been drinking, amused at the ones who have. She takes a glass of water into the sitting room and lies back down on the couch. She holds her arms around a cushion and pretends to sleep, her knees and feet drawn up into the slip.

I walk up the hall to Dickie's room. His long dark shape is in the bed, an open bottle of gin on the table beside him. His clothes are on wire hangers, on a string rigged up along the curtain rod. He's discarded his pillow, a lump on the floor by my feet. I pick it up, a sewn-up linen square with sand in it. It was my pillow when I was a child. My mother made it. I've never seen one like it since. I hug the coarse material against my face. You have to punch a dent for your head before you lie down.

"Callie?" says Dickie with his eyes still closed. I go to the bed, climb quietly over him, sit on his ribs. He doesn't seem to mind my knees on his arms.

"It's Day," I say.

He opens his eyes, his eyebrows are close to his hairline. He doesn't struggle, he's too drunk to fight. He doesn't make sounds, as if he's half expecting me, as though I'm in a dream he's had before. I place the pillow over his face, spread the edges so I can't see his hair.

There's a familiar dullness to the sound, a boy punching a sack of barley that hangs by a rope from the feedshed rafters, safe in the air from mice. But this bag doesn't swing, it's up against his face. The blunt thud of my fist making and remaking its shape. Grains of sand trickle as the stitches spread, down his shoulders and onto the bed, not freely like hourglass sand, but in little cakes and clusters, some in the sweat on my knuckles. A dull pain goes up my arm. It doesn't feel like he's my father.

I look up and see my shadow painted on the wall, the

bend of my arm distorted, the length of my head, my shoulders as wide as half the room. I can't see my expression, just the pillow all over his face, the numbness in my forearm, the burn in my bent-up fingers. His clothes on their hangers stand in the window like long, dark relatives. The air has gone from all around us.

"Day," says Callie from behind me. I try to breathe slowly but my chest is racking. Dickie is still. He looks at me oddly as I uncover him, as if he isn't hurting. His cheeks are scraped and burn-bruised, a split on his lip, smudges of blood from his nose. But his face has kept its shape, he doesn't seem daunted by consequences.

Callie's wrapped in a blanket; she's brought him a glass of cordial. She puts it on the bedside table. He half laughs then stops. "I'm bleeding," he says, "I can taste it." He touches his face, dabs his lip with an index finger. There are patches of sand on his skin.

I pick up his towel from the end of the bed. "Can you dampen it?" he says to Callie. I spit on a corner and hand it to him. My arm is shaking slightly. His face is raked and already swelling, like he's been dragged on gravel.

"I haven't been with her," he says groggily. The word "yet" at the end of the sentence hangs in the silence between us like it's all we have in common.

I reach for the pillow. There are bloodstains on the stitching. I clutch it, like a child might clutch the remains of a toy, and stand at the foot of the bed. Dickie blots his lip with the towel.

"Callie was raped by her father," I say. She squints at

me dimly. It wasn't mine to say, but I hold her look as if I'm entitled. She sits down beside the glass on the bedside table, flushed and confused. I wonder if drinking magnifies the worst in her or if it's closer to who she is.

Dickie turns his head to see her; he seems neither sad nor surprised, only drunk. He doesn't say he's sorry. She leans to him as if about to whisper but looks at the cut on his cheek. He closes his eyes, he's going to sleep.

"Do you want to stay with him?" I ask her.

She shakes her head but it doesn't mean no. She slumps back into the chair.

I walk down the hall to the kitchen, glad to be out of the room. I follow the runner of carpet like I'd otherwise lose my way. I cup my hands and drink from the tap. Water pours from the faucet and into a spoon in the sink, it splashes onto my clothes. I'm the only one who's sober.

The bath is where I come to be alone, the only water I feel safe in. It stays still unless I move it, the sides and bottom are always in reach.

My mother washed me here—"bath washering" she called it. She knelt on a box because the sides were so high, reached in with her soft, soapy hands. They rinsed the farm from my hair. Her thumb pressed a track along my brow, keeping the soap from my eyes. She finger-painted in the soapsuds on my stomach, above where the water stopped. The shape of things I had to guess. An umbrella, a dog, a house on a mountain. I thought it was a pair of hats.

A cool bath on a hot night is like eating cucumbers. In the dark it can transport you. The water takes the itch from my skin, the anger from my hands, the blood back to my feet. I wait for my mind to wander, away from Dickie and Callie. I add hot water but it doesn't mix in. I stir it to distract me.

"Up as far as possible, down as far as possible—now we're washing possible," my mother would say. She would laugh like it was the first time anyone said it. She stopped washing me the day she lost the baby. Tomorrow I'll have to wash Darwin.

I kneel up in the water. The warm night air is cold on my skin. I feel down the outside of the bath to the place against the wall where I'd hide things. Bits of old soap, veiled in cobwebs, a cup for rinsing hair, the cork we used as a plug. I line them up on the ledge like decorations. Sometimes I sit in the bath when it's empty.

Footsteps come light but slow, like my mother's when she ventured in the night. It must be Callie, though her step is usually more precise. She reaches in the air for the string and pulls it. The lightbulb is brown inside, it shows the room dimly. She doesn't notice my clothes on the chair. The sides of the bath keep me from being seen. I move without disturbing the water.

She drags the slip up over her head and puts it in the basin under the running taps. She has nothing on underneath. She soaps then kneads it between her knuckles like she's working something out. She stops and watches it. Her hands grip the sides of the basin as though she might not stand without them. She sits down on the lavatory seat, rests her elbows on her knees. She pees and dabs herself with a piece of paper.

"Do you want a bath?" I ask. She faces me, immodest, her expression doesn't alter, her hands don't cup her opposite shoulders. She seems beyond surprise.

"What are you doing?" she asks.

"Wallowing," I say.

"Why did you let me drink?" she asks.

"I should have had some myself," I say. "We'd have all been asleep by nine o'clock." My laugh sounds brittle. Callie doesn't join me; not in the laughter or in the bath.

"What time is it?" she asks. "I feel awful."

"It must be after two," I say. "Why are you washing the slip?"

"It had stuff on it," she says.

"From dinner?" I ask.

"Grass stains," she says, "from dancing."

"Only green grass leaves stains," I say. "You shouldn't have been out there."

"Good Lord," she says like it's hardly my business. It doesn't sound like her. "Good Lord" is Dickie's expression—when he holds his cigarette wide and lets his head flop back. He says it when things are funny or overdone.

"Did you close your eyes and think of Argentina?"

"We didn't do anything, Day," she says. "He only kissed me."

"He's my father," I say.

Darwin looks up at me warily. He doesn't move or try to speak. He has on a makeshift diaper. I made it for him. A towel with a plastic Superphosphate bag, clipped together with safety pins. He's had it on two days. At first the plastic smelt of fertiliser. Now the smell is different, like ammonia.

"Hospital wash," I say. "Armpits and crotch." I unclip the pins and put them on the bedside table. "It's not the armpits I'm worried about," I say. Darwin snorts through his nose, it might be a laugh. I pull the diaper out from underneath him and put it in a pillowcase. The plastic is wet but not soiled.

He looks small on the bed, his belly is sunken. His rib cage is swollen, yet each of his ribs still shows. He labours each breath but at least they are even. But the air only goes to his chest, it doesn't swell in his belly. I need to keep talking, the sound of my voice keeps the tears from my eyes.

"Remember how you'd feed a raw egg to a calf, make it swallow the shell?" I talk as if those days were fun. I soap the sponge in the bucket and start down his arm. His muscles feel tight and reluctant. "But that was for diarrhoea," I say. I fill the air with words, focus on the freckles on his shoulder, some that are raised and blackened from sun. Dark spots on pale skin.

"I was hoping Leonie would be here for this," I say.

Up as far as possible and down as far as possible. I wash him like it's no big deal. "Did you know I'm circumcised?" I ask him. "They must have done it on the boat." I don't turn him over, I'm afraid he'll fall from the bed.

Callie comes in with a jug of fresh water. I'm glad of the diversion. "I haven't told Darwin what's going on in the rest of the house," I say.

"I've started drinking," she says to Darwin.

I cover him up so she can't see. His feet poke from the end of the sheet, his toenails are ridged and long, but I can't deal with them now. Callie fills a yellow cup with water.

"Would you like some whiskey in it?" she asks him.

"He needs prunes," I tell her.

She leaves the room and goes down the hall. I don't know where she'll find them.

I decide not to tackle his hair. I don't know how I'd wash it without wetting the bed. Instead, I sprinkle powder on it, muss it about so his hair doesn't look so greasy. As I put the tin down, I realise it's tinea powder. "You won't be getting athlete's foot," I tell him.

Callie returns with a plastic kite. "I thought you were looking for prunes," I say. The kite has yellow banners and a red Chinese dragon. "That's mine," I tell her. "I got it one Christmas but there wasn't any wind." The sun was so hot the plastic expanded, it didn't stay taut on its frame.

"I thought we could hang it from the light so Darwin has something to look at," she says. She brings it over and stands on the chair, her paddock boots on the velvet. She doesn't ask him if he wants a kite. I put my knee on the seat to keep it firm, hold her still as she reaches around the hanglight. I steady her hips with my hands and lift her a few inches higher, my face in the small of her back. It feels nice being against her, the smell of her unwashed shirt. I wonder if I'll forgive her.

"Looks good," she says as I let her down. "Brightens up the room." She puts the electric fan on the chair and faces it upwards. The kite pitches and flits without rhythm or logic, like a bird that's trapped inside. The way it angles and dives above Darwin's head is unsettling.

"It's too low," I say. I turn off the fan and get on the chair, try to tie the string shorter.

"Did you hear about Day and Dickie?" Callie says to Darwin. "Day hit him seventeen times." I shorten the string with a series of hitches. Darwin just looks at her. His eye is watery as always. I can't tell if he likes her or not.

"Would you have let Dickie kiss you if you hadn't been drunk?" I ask her. I angle the fan more towards Darwin and not so high up in the air.

Callie looks up at the yellow dragon as it wafts about the room. "It was an accident," she says.

Darwin watches her. His head is shaking slightly. It might be the tremors that old people get, but it looks like disapproval.

Callie shouts my name. I get to the doorway, she's standing by the window. "Dickie's gone," she says. The place in the bed where he slept is empty. She pulls the curtains so we can see in the light. His suitcase isn't there, just a stack of wooden hangers and a *Paris Match* magazine. An empty wineglass lies on the floor, the towel he used to dab his face is folded by the door.

"He's been gone before," I say, as if I'm not concerned. I look out the window towards the scrub but there's no sign of him walking. The Vauxhall is gone from down at the sheds but there is no hint of dust along the road.

"He's taken Darwin's car," I say. "He's been gone a while."

Callie flattens the bed with her hands as if to erase his shape. I can't tell if she's sad that he's left or if she's relieved.

"He left a photo," she says. There are two, neatly placed on the bedside table. A bay polo pony, leather boots on its legs, its tail bandaged up into a stub. "Appeal Book," the horse's name, is written on the bottom, "Windsor, 1952." Beside it is another. Dickie standing where my mother stood, by the fountain in the snow, taken on an angle. You can see the tops of the buildings.

"My mother must have taken this," I say.

In the photo Dickie's wearing a fur hat and pleated gaucho trousers, a zipped-up leather jacket. He's posing with a cigarette in the rain.

"His feet have been cut off," says Callie.

"She should have cut off more than his feet."

I kneel beside Darwin's bed, turn off the fan so his room is quiet. He strains without moving, he can't tell what's happening. "Dickie left," I say.

Darwin juts his neck. His mouth is dry, a whiteness about his tongue.

"He took your car."

The kite sags from the ceiling like an old face. There's something pagan about the stretch of colourful plastic, the red and yellow. Without the fan it just hangs there.

"Will you call the police?" asks Callie from the door.

Darwin shakes his head.

"They'd only find him," I say.

Everything seems more obvious outside on the veranda. I watch Callie walk down into the paddock, through the Patterson's curse. It's as if she's been waiting for something to happen and now it has, but it's not what she expected. I remember how she ran through the trees from the Wye River Road, so quick and light the twigs didn't break. Now the lightness to her movement seems contrived. I searched for her through the blur of the lens on the shore at Rehoboth, as though she might come up from somewhere surprising or stand on a sandbank laughing. She walked up the beach alone. I've tried to get a fix on her, but she shifts like teeth in a gearbox.

I walk down and stand beside her in silence. It's hot in the sun. Flies form islands as they settle on the bright patches of earth. The brindle dog watches from the gate as if by proxy. It feels like days since Dickie and Callie danced in the garden, but it's only been twelve hours.

"Say something," she says. I imagine them kissing, his smoky mouth around hers. I stare at the dun-coloured dirt but I can't think of anything to say. Thinking about it disgusts me; I'm not sorry he's gone. I look over to where the grass has grown over my mother in patches, like a reluctant sore.

"My mother loved him," I say.

Callie squints into the yellow-brown paddock, she

doesn't shade her eyes. "He said I made him feel young," she says.

I kick at a small rock. "I made him feel old."

Callie leans forward to scratch at her calf. Her cheeks are shiny, her skin hasn't dried in the heat. "Dickie understood me," she says.

"He didn't love you." I can tell by the way she turns her head she doesn't want to talk about it more. We walk down towards the billabong.

"What did he understand?" I ask. She takes a long time to answer.

"About my father," she says.

We stand in the sponge of carpetweed that grows at the edge of the water. She picks up a patch of it. "In America we call this baby's tears."

"How do you know that?" I say. She doesn't care about plants and grasses.

"We had a pond near our house," she says.

I pluck a tiny green head from its stem, put it on the point of my finger. I try to blow it into the water but it sticks to my skin. "My mother lost a baby here," I say. "She was teaching me to swim." I take a sheath of the weed to the gum tree, tuck it like a piece of lawn between the roots. "This is where she buried it," I say. "I don't know if it was a boy or a girl. It was Darwin's child." I remember the Star of David made from sticks; the way my mother walked back up to the house. She passed right by me as though I wasn't there.

"After that she didn't take care of herself. She stopped

brushing her hair." Her silver brush and hair clasps left in the dust on her dressing room table. "Then she stopped wearing shoes."

"Darwin lives like it's just after the War," Callie says. I don't know why she says it, she's only seen him lying still.

"He was like that before," I say.

"You care more about him than Dickie," she says.

"Darwin stayed," I say. "He loved her." It feels strange to say it, like a smite or a sacrilege.

Callie throws a rock out into the middle. It makes a hollow sound, the water ripples. The reeds on the bottom beckon like fingers. I don't like the look of it.

"I hope no one ever loves me like that," she says.

I turn away from the water. "I once wanted to be like Dickie," I say. "He taught me how to ride properly." It's strange to imagine him already gone. I make a round shape with my thumb and first finger, put it to my eye as though it is a monocle, the way I did as a child when I watched my mother and Dickie talking in the garden. Darwin watched them too.

"Dickie wasn't that much older than we are now," I say.

I close my other eye and scan the paddock, imagine what it would be like being Darwin, seeing with only one. Everything seems to be magnified. A shovel lies not far from my mother's grave like a rusting piece of evidence. The chicken-wire fence around her stone; the barrow was her cooling board. I look up into the whitening sun. Even the obvious things seem hard to remember.

I sit down at the water's edge. Callie kneels beside me.

I look into her face, her pale brown eyes.

"What do you want from me?" I ask her.

If she thinks she's beautiful she pretends she doesn't. The way her front tooth overlaps just slightly. She hasn't been burnt by the sun.

"To be understood," she says.

"You don't make it easy," I say.

She picks up a twig and draws a stick-figured horse in the sand.

"Will you forgive me?" she asks.

"It's whether I'll trust you."

She draws a fence around the horse and then what looks like a car.

"If I didn't want to be with you I wouldn't be here," she says. She hugs her knees and rests her chin between them. "When I met you," she says, "you were so Australian. Your hair all over your face. It was hard understanding what you were saying. Remember Maryland, going to towns and jumping the car? Hoofers with his hat pulled down?"

"You were only sixteen," I say.

"I liked you then," she says, "but I like you better now."

"You've never told me you love me," I say.

She smooths some ground with her hand, and takes her stick. In big, slow letters she writes: *I DO.* She looks at the words, traces them with her finger as if she's wondering what they mean. She doesn't speak or look at me.

"Do you want to stay?" I ask her.

"Here?" she says.

"Until Darwin dies."

"As long as it's not forever," she says.

I look to the house on the hill. The branches of the Moreton Bay fig form shadows along the veranda. Something moves in Darwin's window. It could be a branch but there isn't a breeze. Callie sees it too. It seems like the window is open and he's sitting up in the bed, watching out as we watch in, straining with his good eye into the bright afternoon.

"It could be a long time," I say.

Callie lays her head on my lap. I play with her hair. It's short and fine like feathers. I never thought of Darwin improving, I always imagined him dead.

"Dickie wants you to have his farm in California," she says.

"How do you know?"

"He told me," she says.

"I could make this into a horse farm," I say. "Get them cheap from the picnic races."

I feel in my pocket for the remnant of my mother's dress, the pale fray in my fingers. I can almost feel the colour.

Callie closes her eyes. Her mouth is open slightly. The sun glistens in the moisture on her crooked tooth, it makes the smallest rainbow. I have the words she's drawn in the dirt. It's more than I imagined.

ACKNOWLEDGMENTS

There are thanks to my grandmother, Aimée Frances Norma Bright, for her stories and early memories of Palparara; to Kathy Kusner for teaching me to ride when I thought I already knew how and for sharing her adventures; to Les Plesko for allowing me to find my voice and guiding me; to Marion Rosenberg for her counsel and encouragement; to Nicholas Pearson at Fourth Estate for his lovely edit of the U.K. edition and to Abner Stein and Nicole Aragi, who are the best; to the Literature Fund of the Australia Council, the Keesing Fellowship, and the Cité Internationale des Arts in Paris; to Lisalee Wells, Don Hunt, David Ebershoff, Stuart Clapp, Ann La Morena, and Meredith Higgins at Fulbright & Jaworski L.L.P. in Los Angeles for their enduring support; to Christel Paris at Éditions du Seuil in Paris for introducing me and the book to MacAdam/Cage; to David Poindexter for his sensibility, humour, and commitment to fiction and new writers, and to Anika Streitfeld for her input and care with the U.S. edition; to Caz Love, Anne Wyman, Marta Ross, Jane Nuñez,

Julianne Cohen, Jane Smiley, Janet Fitch, Jean Wingis, Josh Miller, Jane Deknatel, Ali Deknatel, and Elaine Kagan; to my family, whom I love very much and who are far away—my dear brother, Peter, his wife, Peta, and to Tristan, Josie, and Tim in Jeetho, my mother, Judy, and my father, Derry, and all who help at Tooradin; to my darling sister, Sally, and Miranda too; to my attic in Los Angeles and the view from its window, and to the cemeteries and secret places where I sit with pen in hand and hope for moments when words might come.